HIM HER
HIM *Again*
THE END
of HIM

A NOVEL BY

Patricia Marx

SCRIBNER

New York   London   Toronto   Sydney

SCRIBNER
1230 Avenue of the Americas
New York, NY 10020

SCRIBNER and design are trademarks of
Macmillan Library Reference USA, Inc., used under license
by Simon & Schuster, the publisher of this work.

For information about special discounts for bulk purchases,
please contact Simon & Schuster Special Sales:
1-800-456-6798 or business@simonandschuster.com.

Text set in Bembo

Manufactured in the United States of America

3   5   7   9   10   8   6   4   2

Library of Congress Cataloging-in-Publication Data

Marx, Patricia (Patricia A.)
Him, her, him again, the end of him: a novel/Patricia Marx.
p. cm.
1. Single women—Fiction. I. Title.
PS3563.A756H56 2007
813'.54—dc22
2006044392

ISBN-13: 978-0-7432-9623-6
ISBN-10: 0-7432-9623-0

For

Richard Avedon, Richard Marx, and Gordon Lish

Part 1

HIM

ONE

I was in high school when I read *The Bell Jar* and thought it was about a lucky girl who wins a contest and gets to go to Europe. But what about Sylvia Plath's trying to drown herself? After she strings herself up and before she swallows pills? To tell you the truth, I don't think I looked at that part.

To tell you the truth, I must have skipped a lot of parts in that book, maybe even the whole thing, because, let's see, for starters, it takes place in New York.

Nevertheless: Sylvia Plath finally did get to go to Europe. She studied at Cambridge University in England, and years after I read her book—or rather, some of her book—so did I. While I was there, a collection of Plath's letters to her mother was published, which my mother read and wrote to me about. "Why can't you write letters to me like that?" she asked. "They're so warm and loving."

When I finally read the letters, long after I'd left Cambridge, I discovered that my mother was right. Sylvia Plath's letters *were* warm and loving. "Your mother is always right," my grandmother once told me, "although I have never liked the yellow table in her center hall." My grandmother also told me that she—my grandmother—believes everyone has a determined number of footsteps to use up in a lifetime, and, therefore, it is foolhardy to exercise since you will only exhaust your quota sooner and die.

Let me give you the gist of a typical Plath letter: "My dearest of Mothers, I met the most marvelous man at the Trinity May Ball, where I wore an ice blue gown that was simply divine. Tomorrow, tea with the Queen! I love you!"

I, too, had met a pretty marvelous man in England, though none of my letters home mentioned him. Let me give you the gist of one of those letters: "It's so cold here. And if you like the weather, you'll *LOVE* the food. Do you remember what I'm supposed to be writing my thesis about? I have to hand a chapter in, but I can't remember what my topic is. I think I wrote the title in a postcard I wrote to you a couple of months ago. The bursar's office says they never received your check."

Sylvia Plath and I had one thing in common besides our outfits for socializing with the Queen—mine being a never-worn, never-to-be-worn drab long skirt; and hers, well, to be honest, I can't actually say if she had an ice blue gown or ever met the Queen. As I told you, I was giving you the gist. In any case, Sylvia and I were alike in that both of us had a habit of shielding our mothers, and in my case, my father, too, from what was really going on in our respective lives. You know, of course, about Sylvia's despair and the conclusive oven thing. Even her mother knows now. But I don't think you know very much about me.

An only child, I was born in the suburbs of Philadelphia, a town called Abington. My ancestors were—no, don't worry. I won't tell you *everything*. I'll start when he knocked on my door.

The marvelous man was wearing a rugby shirt and jeans and

sneakers and he looked boyish, I thought, for someone from another generation.

"You don't look twenty-eight," I said. I was twenty-one.

"You can count the rings," he said.

"You're married?" I said. He laughed.

"I meant tree rings," he said. "It was a joke about dendrochronology."

"Oh," I said. "I never get dendrochronological jokes."

He told me that he'd arrived from New York that morning, that he was going to be a teaching fellow in philosophy, that he'd recently been at Princeton, where he studied with someone famous I pretended to have heard of, that he'd taken a year off to join VISTA and eradicate poverty in Scarsdale (did I really hear him say Scarsdale?), and that a friend of mine had suggested he look me up—he'd dated one of her roommates, who'd run off to an ashram in India after he broke up with her. She still wrote to him, though the motif, he said, was mainly gastrointestinal.

Those were the days when a person with a knapsack might knock on your door, say he was a friend of a friend of a cousin of an ex-girlfriend of a guy he had hiked with in Australia, and you then invited this person to sleep on your sofa and eat your food for as long as he felt like it. It was well within your guest's rights to take or break one of your cherished possessions, and unacceptable for you to care because that would be materialistic. Hitchhiking through Europe a year or so before, I had pulled that stunt in Amsterdam and ended up living for a week with someone who'd been a medical student for the last twelve years, during which time he'd saved the rind of every tangerine he'd eaten. Thousands of dried rinds, each a perfect half sphere, were stacked throughout the apartment. Toward the end of my stay, the rinds nearly burned to a crisp when I stood too close to the fireplace and my cheap pants burst into flame.

But Eugene Obello was only wondering if I'd like to go for a walk with him. Right now. Those were also the days before date books and plans and pretending you had something else to do in order to look popular. So I said yes.

While Eugene was in the bathroom, I took one of my smart-looking social theory books from my bookshelf and positioned it in a conspicuous spot. How far I had come from Abington High. "Remember Abington," the principal used to announce every morning over the PA. "First in the alphabet, first in achievement, and first in attitude!" We might have been first in the alphabet, but the other two . . . iffy.

And look at me now: Cambridge University! Abington was a large bland redbrick public high school built in the 1950s. This place was a dominion of majesty established in the thirteenth century by King Henry III. "I'm living like royalty," I wrote to my parents when I arrived. "Could you please send me my down quilt?"

Grungy-looking students hung out all day in the college bar, smoking hand-rolled cigarettes and drinking ale. Another clique modeled itself on the Bloomsbury group—someone dressed and talked like Virginia Woolf, another like Clive Bell, another like Duncan Grant, and so on. There were some actual descendants of the Bloomsbury group at the college, but the look-alikes would have nothing to do with them, regarding them as poseurs. Even the student council was something to write home about: they issued a statement coming out against political, economic, and legal discrimination, which they happened to "deplore."

On the other hand, the school was still mostly made up of upper-class males, the first females having been accepted only a few years earlier. Some of the upper-class males belonged to a society whose sole function, so far as I could make out, was to break into the room of a first-year student, interfere with it, and leave a check for damages done. Then they peed in the fountain—the one topped by a statue of Henry VI with the symbolic figures of Learning and Religion seated below.

So: the splendid architecture, the adorable boys' choir, the fields of daffodils . . . you get it. "They even have grazing cows on the lawns. How inspirational!" I wrote to my parents. "And I heard that only the students in *MY* college are allowed to shoot and eat the swans that swim on the Cam." In a P.S., I added, "I *NEED* money to go to Wales. Maybe you could sell my charm bracelet—the one you gave me for my Sweet Sixteen? It's just a worldly object. Also, could you send me some hangers?"

That entire first year, gosh, I was happy. I was a foreigner! I'd never been to Europe and now here I was, in a country where everyone sounded like Winston Churchill or Mary Poppins; where all the women had flawless skin and all the men looked as if they'd been wandering around in the Underground since World War II, never having seen the light of day or another change of clothes. Every aspect of life in England seemed a notch from normal. Which made even the mundane exotic and exhilarating. I swear if I had been mugged on a greensward, this, too, would have been utterly delightful because he wouldn't have been just any mugger; he would have been a mugger with an accent.

You know what else is nice about being a foreigner? Whatever you do takes place in a capsule that need not be discovered and opened by someone back home. Nothing really counts—it was the life that falls in the forest. That's how I looked at it. I felt free to . . . oh, I don't know.

Eugene returned to my bedroom. He'd been in the bathroom. "If it's not too rude to ask," he said, "bearing in mind I met you only a few minutes ago, and I hope I'm not entering some kind of kinky area here, or maybe I do"—Eugene smiled, I didn't—"but what are all those buckets and funnels doing in your bathtub?" I dropped my lip gloss into a drawer so he wouldn't catch me trying to look good while he'd been out of the room. Makeup seemed like cheating to me, then; but boy, oh boy, it doesn't now.

"I make ginger beer," I said.

Eugene took off his jacket and put it on my bed. "I lay a wager you didn't know that you can simulate ginger ale by combining Sprite with a splash of Coca-Cola," he said.

I picked up Eugene's jacket, looked around, considered what to do with it, put it back on the bed. "Really?" I said. Eugene stared at me while I thought hard what to say. "Sprite seems tough to make," was what I came up with.

"I'm not particularly fond of ginger beer," he said.

"Oh, I hate it," I said, wanting him to think we had an opinion in common. Incidentally, it was true. "But it's easy to make."

Why was a PhD-track graduate student who hated ginger beer involved with moonshine? Because my next-door neighbor, Obax Geeddi Abtidoon, a rich and beautiful Somalian who wanted to be a chef but was getting her degree in polar studies when she wasn't cooking curry and making sliced carrot salad for everyone on the floor, had given me the ginger beer starter and how could I be so rude as to throw it out?

Eugene sat on the only chair. His way of sitting there was so relaxed it put me on edge. Plus, this left the bed as the only place to sit, which seemed too friendly, but I perched myself on the edge anyway and tried to look nonchalant.

I know I said that the buildings at Cambridge were magnificent, but my dorm, built in the sixties out of concrete, was the exception. When I was happy, I found the room sterile and claustrophobia-inducing and depressing; when I was unhappy, I found the room sterile and claustrophobia-inducing and consoling. It was decorated, if that is the word, in basic dormitory furniture but with a touch of a color that could only be called veal—veal curtains, veal bedspread, and a veal and gray shag rug. Instead of wallpaper, the walls were covered with grainy veal linoleum—linoleum was definitely a theme in this building. A mechanical alarm clock sitting on a bookshelf was wrapped in a towel because someone had told me that fluorescence caused multiple myeloma. On the floor cartons of books lay, which I had insisted my parents ship to me because I believed I couldn't live without being surrounded by literature. I shipped them home every summer when I returned to Philadelphia and they came back with me every fall. I don't think I ever opened one, but this was a phase of my life when I wrote things in letters to my parents such as "I'm reading a lot of epistemology because I never had the chance in college," and, "Saw *The Birthday Party* last night in London. I could write like Pinter but when would I get around to it with this damn thesis around my neck?"

My room overlooked a courtyard in which there was a small man-made pond stocked with goldfish. After a potted gardenia I had placed on my windowsill fell into the pond, it seemed by volition, I went around saying that flowers committed suicide when they were near me. From my window, I could see my friend Libby's room, on the same floor. She and I constantly wrote notes, slipping them underneath one another's door. Libby was an undergraduate studying Anglo-Saxon, Norse, and Celtic, so her notes were, as she said, "strewn with rune." In a letter home, I compared Libby's wit with that of P. G. Wodehouse, though I had never read a single book of his.

"Let **N** represent the set of natural numbers," Eugene said.

"If it's up to me," I said, "**N** can be anything it wants."

"Very good," Eugene said. "Now let's put forth the proposition that there cannot be a set of all sets. And yet it seems also true that any group of items can be collected into a set, right?"

I nodded. It couldn't be possible—could it?—that upper-echelon philosophers were doing the same math that Miss Kilroy taught us in third grade?

I'd asked Eugene to explain what he was working on, a little bit because I wanted to know but mostly because I wanted to divert him long enough for me to walk over to the window and discreetly arrange the curtains so they obscured the sealed bottle of milk that had been sitting on my sill for about three months. I didn't know much about much, but something told me that putrefying milk was not the way to put one over on a suitor. I must have intuitively known even then, though, that if you ask a certain type of guy about himself, it's as good as winding a wind-up toy. For a given amount of time, said guy is in motion and requires only minimal attention from you. In this way, men are easier than plants.

"You really want to hear this?" he said.

"Yes!" I said.

The bottle, by the way, was an experiment, albeit one without a hypothesis. My research partner, Libby, and I were simply curious to see what would happen to very, very, very old milk. So far, blue and green had happened.

Let's now ignore Eugene while he describes what he's working on, throwing around some Greek symbols in the process. Meanwhile, I'll tell you what I was working on. Eugene had not asked, so it hadn't come up in our conversation.

Nothing.

In April, the month I met Eugene, my thesis topic, an ever-changing thing, had something to do with comparing the Jewish struggle against Fascism in the 1930s in Britain with the West Indian struggle against racism and the National Front today. The problem with that, it turned out, was they had almost nothing in common. My original topic had been "The Effects of the Changing Role of Women in a Yorkshire Fishing Village Upon Family and Social Structure." However, after I'd spent several weeks in an actual Yorkshire fishing village, interviewing dozens of people, it became clear that because of their accent I had no idea what anyone was saying. Transcripts of the hundred or so hours of tapes reveal that I frequently asked my subjects questions they'd just answered. And they were so polite. They answered again.

Whatever the topic, I was not working on it. Instead, I spent my time . . . come to think of it, I had turned into one of those people of whom I think, What *do* they do all day?

Let's see. Leafing through brochures of Mediterranean islands to which I would never travel took time, as did my daily swim in the public pool across town. Then there were the excursions to the nearest department store to try on cashmere sweaters; to the open-air market to buy a mere satsuma orange. I taught myself to ride a bicycle without using hands and tried to teach myself German from a book, mastering only the phrase for "You are a fried egg" before I quit. I went to the Black Kettle across the street, where my work-shy friends and I lingered over cups of coffee for the sole purpose of eavesdropping on the inane conversations of tourists. (Man, pointing to the steps to the second floor of the restaurant; to waiter: "Do these stairs go up?") I made frequent visits to the stationery store to buy everything in sight. "Can you believe it?!" I wrote my parents. "This country has no double yellow adhesive labels! Please send some."

That's what I did all day, and curiously, nobody in a position of authority much cared. Two months had passed since I'd seen my adviser, Geoffrey Guppy, a genial man in his sixties, known for his work in the tribal politics of Guinea-Bissau and also in the sociology of what transpires during the first minute of conversation in different cultures. We'd met to discuss a chapter I'd written entitled "How Successful is T. S. Kuhn in

Avoiding Problems of Relativism in His Discussion of Paradigms in Natural Sciences," for a thesis whose topic I can't conjure up today or perhaps even then. But I do remember his critique: "I looked up the word 'redeive,' " he had said, "and couldn't find it in the dictionary."

"It was a typo," I had said. "I meant 'receive.' "

"Jolly good. Carry on. Now. When you write 'in 1934,' do you mean 'in the *year* 1934'?"

There is nothing else in the English language that "in 1934" could possibly mean, but I kept that to myself. A week later, Geoffrey Guppy departed for Guinea-Bissau to do research and I was given a stand-in, Sean Shanahan, a scholar of revolution, who liked sherry and gossip. He believed that students were adults and should be treated as such, which meant he had affairs with some of them, though not with me. It also meant that he never broached the subject of my thesis. Geoffrey Guppy never returned to Cambridge, so don't worry about keeping track of his name. Sean Shanahan remained my temporary adviser forever. He will prove to be of only minor significance in this story. If you forget his name, I'll remind you the next time it comes up.

If a teacher believes that a certain undergraduate is not sharp enough to cut it in academia, is it the teacher's responsibility to dissuade said student from continuing his or her education, thereby saving the student money and time, or should the teacher respect the student's autonomy and simply hope that he or she will figure it out eventually?

Eugene and I began discussing this issue when he mentioned that a student of his from Princeton had recently asked for advice about applying to graduate schools. Eugene considered the student mediocre.

"You told him he was stupid?!" I said.

"I used a different word," Eugene said. " 'Obtuse.' "

"And what did he say?" I said.

"He said thank you," Eugene said. "He must have been thinking of 'astute.' "

Eugene and I were still in my room, though we hadn't been there as long as you probably think, maybe a half hour. We were having instant coffee, which I found delicious because it was Dutch. It didn't bother me that the coffee contained specks of crud—all the more bohemian. I later realized I'd been drinking metal fragments from the electric kettle. I am including this detail in case I get a mysterious disease and the doctors need help with the diagnosis.

"You said he had a B-plus average at Princeton," I said. "How obtuse could he be?" Was there a way, I strained to think, to work in the fact without seeming to brag that I, too, had a commendable college grade point average?

"To make a career in philosophy you have to be brilliant," said the person who was making his career in philosophy.

"He could be a late bloomer. You never know," said the person who was beginning to fear she was an overachiever mistaken for an underachiever.

"Believe me," he said, stirring his coffee, "you can tell everything from day one."

"Isn't that playing God?" I said, thinking the phrase was sophisticated. I was also thinking that I should probably tell Eugene, still stirring away, that those were specks of crud, not lumps of coffee, in his coffee.

"I don't believe in God," he said. "And if I *were* a believer, I certainly wouldn't believe in deism." Deism? What did deism have to do with it? I was out of my league. "Maybe French deism, but certainly not the deism of Holingbroke or Locke,"

Eugene said. Does that clarify anything for you? Because it didn't for me. Then again, as I said, I was out of my league.

"Well, it's still cruel," I said.

"Honesty, in the long run, is always kindest," Eugene said. He set his mug on the bed table and was done with it.

Our conversation was rife with ironies and I missed them all. One always does when everything is going well. "Then again," Eugene said, "you know, of course, what Nietzsche said about lying?" This is what I came to Cambridge for, I thought: stimulating intellectual conversation.

There are two ways to deal with an awkward pause. You can fill the void by babbling or you can suppose it's the other person's fault and wait it out. Hold on. There's a third approach. You can exploit the opportunity and make a sexual advance. I was afraid that Eugene would go for that, so I preemptively asked him, "Are there any rivers in Nebraska?" Eugene had grown up in Missouri.

"There's the Niobrara River, obviously," said Eugene, "and the Platte River and the Missouri River and the Republican River and the Loup River, both the North Loup and the South Loup." Eugene picked up his knapsack. He had that gearing-up-to-say-good-bye look.

"Yeah, yeah," I said, "I mean besides those? Tributaries." Eugene got up. "Or maybe byways," I said. That might have been the end of him for me. I had an awful suspicion that a byway was a minor road, having nothing to do with a river. But the door opened.

"You're here!" said Libby, meaning me, not Eugene. Standing next to her was a guy I'd never seen before and, instantly, I understood what had happened. When I had adjusted my curtains to hide the bottle of milk, I'd inadvertently arranged them in a way that sent Libby, who—remember?—could see my window from hers, a message that I was leaving and she could use my room for entertaining. Our elaborate semaphore system, based on which lights were on and how the curtains were drawn, included code for "Trying to work. Please disturb"; "Wake me up by noon"; "I'm drunk. Do you have aspirin? What day is it?"; and "I just thought of another reason I despise Tamar Grubley." Libby's room, by the way, was too messy for trysts.

I know you're thinking: Ewwww, lending out your room for *that?* But we had illicit keys to the closet where housekeeping kept fresh linen. And lest you think I got the short end of the deal, I should mention that Libby allowed me the use of her computer (mine had crashed without warning) and whatever else was in her room while she was at lectures, the library, and engaged in other studious activities. Libby was able to play and work whereas I couldn't do either. But my room was neat. And I had to get out of it immediately.

I grabbed Eugene's arm. "This is Eugene," I said with haste, "and he and I are going for a walk."

We walked along the gravel path that squared the Front Court of the college, a large turf of grass that had been perfectly tended for well over five hundred years. Then we cut the corner and walked on the grass, though signs in many languages clearly stated, KEEP OFF THE GRASS UNLESS YOU ARE A FELLOW OF THE COLLEGE! It doesn't sound thrilling, but believe me, it was.

We continued down the path, past a grand building that looked like a little nation's capitol. When we made our way to the Back Lawn, I was glad to be noticed by a show-off who had gone to college with me in the United States and was using every last pence of her National Science Foundation Fellowship to buy upmarket wine. Eugene was terrific-looking and I knew she'd be jealous.

(At this point, I think it behooves me to tell you what

Eugene looked like. But description is the part I skip when I read a book, so let's just leave it that he was terrific-looking, okay? And kind of, well, nondescript. If you really care what color his hair was or whether his eyes were shaped like almonds or pistachios, write to me and I'll send you a picture.)

But here's the more important part: we were also noticed on the Back Lawn by Oliver Qas (pronounced like the French word for "what"). Oliver Qas was a theologian in his second year from Trinidad, who was maybe more terrific-looking than Eugene and with whom I'd almost had a fling when I arrived in Cambridge and who flourished a walking stick. I could count on Oliver saying hello in a flirty way and he did. "If it isn't the toast of two hemispheres," he said.

On the other hand, I was not glad to be noticed by Laurence Hesseltine, a rabbity-looking English third-year studying artificial intelligence, who'd been chosen by Stephen Hawking as one of the undergraduates whose job it was to push him around in his wheelchair and guess what he was saying. Laurence saw me and waved, bending his fingers as if he were waving to a baby. I started to wave back but in midgesture worried that this might encourage Laurence, who had never spoken to a girl, to speak to me, so I combed my fingers through my hair as if that had been my intention all along.

Eugene noticed none of these people. He was explaining the sorites paradox, also known as the heap paradox. "One grain of sand isn't a heap," he said. I kicked a stone. "And if you add one more grain of sand, it still isn't a heap, do you follow?"

Eugene and I caught up with the stone and I kicked it again.

"If you add a third grain of sand," Eugene said, "it still isn't a heap. And so forth ad infinitum. It seems, then, that there can be no such thing as a heap of sand. Yet, we know there is. Which is why it's called a paradox."

"The heap paradox," Eugene said, "was at the root of a lot of debates—when is a fetus a living being, when is the budget too high, when do you pull your troops out of a war that seems a lost cause? Where do you draw the line?"

I did some more stone kicking. "Do you know the book *Seven Types of Ambiguity*?" I said, referring to a book they had made me read in school. I had a vague hunch it was relevant to what Eugene was talking about. I needed Eugene to think that I was smart.

Eugene nodded. "William Empson," he said.

"Don't you think a better title would be *Seven or Eight Types of Ambiguity*?" I said. I needed Eugene to think I was clever, too. Eugene chuckled.

We had come to the Backs, the strip of land that was on the side of the Cam opposite to my dorm. The Cam, lined with willow trees, was closer to a creek than a river, but beautiful. Students and tourists glided by in punts. The lawns were covered with daffodils and those little purple flowers that I think are called crocuses. The sun was setting. I thought, This is what I'm supposed to think is romantic. Now Eugene kicked the stone.

We stood, facing each other. He fixed his eyes on me and I wondered what was next. How do two people move from talking to not talking to doing it? He raised his hand. Was he going to kiss me? Then he scratched his shoulder. I have to tell you the idea of what might happen made me anxious, which may explain why I was, as I will later demonstrate, the least experienced twenty-one-year-old, if you don't count Mormons, who, come to think of it, are probably married by twenty-one, so scratch that. At least, I thought, Eugene didn't look like a man. He looked my age, or even younger.

"Did any presidents come from Missouri?" I said.

TWO

Before I forget, I must tell you that the guy Libby brought to my room turned out to be the heir to the Weetabix fortune. Weetabix is the number-one cereal manufacturer in Great Britain. A couple of days after Libby and the heir met, she returned to her room from breakfast and found it jam-packed with boxes of Weetabix, Weetabix Banana Mini-Crunch, Alpen Caribbean Crunch, Alpen Nutty Crunch, Alpen Blackberry & Apple, Instant Ready Brek, Strawberry and Yogurt Bars, and Choco-rrific Wheatos. We don't know how he managed to get into her room, but we figured he paid off the head porter. There were no boxes of Alpen Original, Libby's favorite, and she wanted to ask for some, but since she had no intention of seeing the heir ever again, I convinced her to skip it.

This was typical Libby. I don't mean guys always gave her grain products. I mean that she had incredible allure. Even Laurence Hesseltine was so bewitched he followed Libby around for months, goo-goo eyed. Finally, he mustered up the guts to say, "Would one like to have a cup of coffee with me?" She obliged.

I am probably the last person who could tell you exactly what it was about Libby that grabbed hold of guys, but unfortunately, I am the only person you know who knew her. She was seductive, I think, because she loved men; all men—she wasn't picky. Who else would even have touched Pip Summerland III, who snacked on dog food? Or Tibor Wike, who argued fiercely about everything from how to wear a college scarf to the existence of Satan, only to signal the end of a debate by falling asleep, suddenly and profoundly? Libby's success might also have had something to do with her fluency. If you know six languages, it's easy to pick up a seventh. Same with men for Libby. Men flocked to her because men flocked to her. Also, she had big you-know-whats.

None of this applied to me.

Two nights after Eugene didn't kiss me in the Fellows Garden, we went to see *State of the People* at the Arts Cinema, which we'd chosen over *Strip Nude Before Your Killer* at the Victoria Theatre because the Arts allowed patrons to book tickets over the phone. And in case you're wondering what exactly did happen in the garden: we'd run into the dean of the chapel, who lectured Eugene and me about the nonalignment of certain chancels with their naves, sort of wrecking the mood for us. I was partly relieved.

As it turned out, the movie was relevant to me since, at the time, I was a neo-Marxist and, along with many of my friends, felt that Trotskyism was old-fashioned and Maoism . . . I can't remember what was wrong with Maoism but it was definitely infra dig, though I secretly loved that Little Red Book. Don't, however, presume I was against money. "I didn't deposit the check you sent," I wrote to my parents, "because someone told me the pound was going to drop. The pound went *up* 2.8 cents! I lost about $14! Speaking of money, would you be willing to give me extra for my birthday if I promise not to hitchhike? There's a killer loose in East Anglia."

Anyway, during the arson sequence in *State of the People*, Eugene put his arm around me and whispered "Stellar!" I took the arm as a compliment but not the "stellar." After the movie, back in my room, we drank Lipton tea with powdered cream, ate McVities digestive biscuits, and went over the pros and cons of stressing the first syllable rather than the second in "hegemony."

"Are you aware," said Eugene, walking purposively toward me, "that a few dissenting scholars pronounce it with a *g*"—he leaned over and kissed the top of my head, then pulled back, looking me straight in the eye—"that is hard?" I realize that probably sounds stupid, but it didn't at the time. Eugene looked as if he was going to kiss me again, possibly on the lips this time.

Here's what I was thinking: This better not be like the last time someone kissed me.

That fiasco had taken place my first night in England. I'd like to blame it all on jet lag but no amount of fatigue gets me off the hook. Here's what happened: Oliver Qas—the guy who said I was the toast of two hemispheres—had made himself known to me at the get-together that the social and political science department was throwing for new students. The party, if that's what you wanted to call it, was held in the department common room, a small space lit with flickering discount lamps and furnished with plastic tables and nonmatching plastic chairs, all of which looked as if it had been left over from a tag sale. Most of the students congregated by the cheese, consuming more Cheddar than one ought to at 11 P.M. Or any time.

When Oliver Qas appeared, I'd been trying to get away from a Fiona something, who was throwing back paper cups of wine as she described the methodology for her study of the British Civil Service in India during the years 1933 to 1935. "I have a floor-to-ceiling map of the country," she said. "Green pushpins represent subjects I've interviewed, red pushpins represent subjects I plan to interview as soon as I can locate them, yellow pushpins represent subjects who are dead or blind, blue pushpins—"

"Must come straightaway to my rooms for vodka and such," said Oliver Qas, taking my arm and sweeping me away from Fiona, who had designs to make her way through the entire color spectrum. Oliver had long black curls, and a sculpted body you could learn anatomy from. (I know I said I was against description—and I really am—but here I'm quoting Libby.) Oliver was wearing white tails as a "delightful little treat" for the guests. The guests were dressed in grub. Oliver was a second-year student who studied hermeneutics, I think because most people didn't know what it was. Also, because he thought it was about getting stoned.

He led me up the winding staircase of a musty building the color of the *Financial Times,* with leaded-glass windows, arched ceilings, and large rooms that overlooked the river. You would pay a lot of money to live in a building like this, despite its being cold and damp and having no doorman. We walked to the top floor and entered the living room by way of an unlocked door. There was a leatherlike sofa, a furlike rug, and a real-glass bong. I wondered what someone so suave was doing with someone so unsuave, someone whose father had said to her when she was fifteen and had not yet tried marijuana, "If I met someone your age who hadn't tried marijuana, I would think there was something wrong."

In one supersonic motion, Oliver Qas took off his shirt and pants. He took a puff on the bong and looked at me expectantly. "I don't think I want to do this," I said, feeling presumptuous to suggest that he in fact had wanted to do something. What if he said he was just hot? It was a chance I had to take.

"Oh, rot," he said. I didn't know what he meant, but I knew enough not to ask.

"I'm kind of involved with someone in America," I said, looking away tragically.

"That's rubbish." He was on to something. Nobody was less involved with someone in America or anyone anywhere else in the world than I was.

"No, really," I said. "We kind of made a pact to not see other people, I think. A six-month trial. We're right in the middle of it. Also, I have to unpack."

Oliver shrugged. "See you about, then," he said blithely and gave me a chummy kiss on the cheek. He turned and walked into his bedroom.

Where I went from Oliver Qas's is anyone's guess. My sense of direction is so bad that in order to figure out which direction is, for example, west, I must mentally lay out a map of the United States in my brain and take note which side California is on. Moreover, I had arrived in Cambridge only about fourteen hours earlier. And so I immigrantishly roamed the grounds of the college in darkness, searching for my dorm or another human being. I would have sworn I had walked to the end of the earth, but in fact had probably crisscrossed a fairly small area closed in by a gate. Finally, I happened upon the porter's lodge. It was locked, though, for after 2 A.M. the night porter went to bed and anyone wishing to pass through the gates had to wake him up. This I was disinclined to do, given that I had no idea whether I was meant to be going to or from.

Oliver did not look surprised to see me standing at his door. He had no clothes on.

"I was thinking about it," I said, "and I decided that actually, I would like to go to bed." I paused, then clarified, "With you."

"Splendid," he said. I noticed that there was now a fire in the fireplace and then I noticed that on the furlike rug, there was another naked person.

"Would you excuse us?" Oliver Qas said to William Bright Brunt, a third-year student who, when he wasn't au naturel, gallivanted around posing as Lytton Strachey, though his beard was merely a loose interpretation of the original and though Strachey, in point of fact, had been a student of a different college. William patted Oliver on the shoulder, then withdrew to the bedroom, where I gather he'd been when I was in the living room the first time.

There was that expectant look again. No two ways about it, I was going to have to take my clothes off, and the scrunched-up tartan blanket on the floor was going to be of no help. I did some calculation: it would take me longer to take off my top (three items) than my bottom (two items that could, if necessary, be removed as one), so starting with the former would minimize the amount of time I would be totally exposed. Then again, if I started with the bottom, there would be less for him to look at for a longer amount of time, and besides, I could sort of crouch.

Now it is time, I think, to tell you, if you haven't already guessed, that at age twenty-one, I had never done it. It was just one of those things, like real estate ads, that I wasn't interested in until later in life.

I may have been indifferent to strong, restless desire in my youth, but not to anxiety. As a teenager, I prepared for the inevitable by studying scenes from movies to determine which way the girl angled her head when she kissed the boy. What I discovered was that, pretty much always, the female, and, therefore, the male, too, tilted to the right. My theory is that it has something to do with the exigencies of cinematic lighting or the fact that most people are right-handed or maybe even the rotation of the earth.

Here goes nothing, I thought, yanking my sweater above my head.

"What about your boyfriend?" Oliver Qas said casually.

"What boyfriend? I don't have a boyfriend," I said, trying to disentangle my barrette from my sweater while trying to preserve my dignity and also not let my midriff look bulgy. "Oh, right. Him," I said, remembering that I did have a fake boyfriend. "We're not technically going out anymore. The six-month pact was just a promise thing."

Under the pretext of helping me with my barrette, Oliver Qas stuck his tongue into my mouth.

I stepped back. "I can't. I just can't. I really like you, but I never have, and you know, no offense, okay? It's just that I'm a . . . you know."

Oliver looked unfazed. "You're going to have to do it sooner or later and it might as well be with me," he said, taking a bossy step in my direction.

"You're right," I said, "but it's just that I'm too tied to my boyfriend right now. Emotionally, I mean," and then I tripped over the tartan blanket. I couldn't help but notice that the plaid was based in white, which my mother told me a plaid never should be.

We parted in good spirits. Lytton Strachey even wrote out directions to my dorm, which he handed to me, before chucking my chin.

And now, Eugene was about to kiss me.

This time, I was ready, and not just psychologically. The day after I had met Eugene, I made an appointment with Dr. Bevan, the doctor who, according to Libby, had killed Ludwig Wittgenstein by misdiagnosing his prostate cancer as malaise until it was too late. "Contraception is not called for, old girl," Dr. Bevan told me. Dr. Bevan emphatically believed that the solution to all physical and mental problems of old girls was pregnancy. "It straightens everything out," he said, on medical authority, I presume.

There was, on the other hand, Dr. Dansie at the Family Planning Clinic, who was to diaphragms as the Avon Lady is to samples. She handed them out enthusiastically to one and all. "Take this with you everywhere," Dr. Dansie said, referring to the practice diaphragm she had given me until she could provide a customized one. "Let's say you're going on a first date; take it along. Or you're going to the beach with an old friend; take it along. Business trip with your boss? Take it along. Lunch with a favorite uncle? My point is that you simply never know which encounter will, ahem, count."

I'm not sure why I told you this since I never even opened the vinyl case that night. How could I? Once things got going, to the extent they got going, it would have seemed, I felt, vexing to interrupt. Besides, I was concerned, above all, that Eugene not figure out that this was my first time and how much more blatant a clue is there than a *practice* diaphragm?

When Eugene kissed me, he tilted his head to the right, though admittedly, I might have forced the position. I kissed him back. Twice. "Your kisses are so recondite, my peach," Eugene said, "that they are almost notional." Until that moment, I had believed I knew the definition of "notional." I had looked it up many times before. Look it up again, I thought, trying not to let the word get in the way of my concentration. "You are to be commended for your artlessness," Eugene said. That was the opposite effect I was going for, but a compliment's a compliment, I thought. Or would that depend on what "notional" meant?

"Beginner's luck," I said, because truth masquerading as a joke is always what I strive for. I needed a short break, so I pretended I had to scratch my nose. That wasn't a long enough break, so I brushed a strand of hair out of my eyes, tucked in my blouse, adjusted my watchband, picked at my nail, plucked some lint off my sweater, got an eyelash out of my eye, cleared my throat, and coughed.

I saw Eugene smile faintly, then put on a serious face. "Shall we, my precious abecedarian . . . proceed?" Eugene solemnly said and just as solemnly, I nodded. Talk about proceeding, my suitor had me on the bed before I knew which end was up. But then the proceeding stopped so that he could amorously fold each item of his clothes, taking special care with the trouser creases, and stack one piece on top of the other on the bedside chair, ending with his socks. He laid his watch on one sock and his eyeglasses on the other. I tried to ignore this preliminary activity, thinking that to take notice constituted prying, in the same way you're not supposed to see what's going on backstage before the show begins.

Unfortunately, I was so intent on coming across as experienced I didn't focus on the experience. I can tell you, though, that the mood was grave, as if we were in the operating room performing high-risk surgery. When Eugene said, in a hushed tone, "Have you a pillow to sustain my neck?" he might as well have said, "Nurse, scalpel."

Later, call it seventeen minutes, we were still under the covers, still undressed, but now we were discussing what it means for one to devote oneself to the Life of the Mind. By that time, I had turned into two people. Number One was lying next to Eugene, faking an interest in what he was saying. Number Two was somewhere else, looking at Number One in stunned disbelief that she had done what she had done, that she had pulled it off. Number Two gloated over Number One's triumph, but worried that perhaps she had not pulled it off. What if Number One had made some mistakes, Number Two thought, and Eugene was too lofty-minded to have pointed them out? Number Two was the one I identified with.

"As I have been noting in my journal—" Eugene stopped abruptly. "For the love of Zeus, deuce it!" he said, shooting out of bed. "How could I be so daft?" As Eugene put on his clothes, he explained that he had left his journal uncovered on his desk at the office and was worried that someone on the cleaning crew might read it. "I had been puzzling over a proof of the Schlendorff Conjecture for Irrational Numbers, and, keep your fingers crossed, seem to be on the verge of cracking it." Eugene crossed his fingers. "My work is not yet ready to show the world," he said, and he planted his finger on his lips, I guess to indicate not another peep about his equations.

Eugene walked backward down the hall, facing me. "Good night," I said.

"How can there be night, my orbital core, when you are not in the sky?" Eugene said, continuing to back slowly away from me.

"Guess I'll go to sleep now," I said. What else could I say?

"You sleep," Eugene said. "And I'll dream." I thought he had put his hand on his heart, but it turned out he was reaching for a mint.

Struggling to believe the heart-first, mint-as-afterthought theory, I said, "Good-bye, Gene." I figured that conveyed affection without seeming cheeky.

Eugene stopped in his tracks. I saw him sucking on the mint. "Perhaps Genie or Hugh or Yoo-hoo," Eugene said, "but never Gene."

Many years later, when Eugene and I had come apart, I mentioned to him that he had been the first for me. Wouldn't you think that that would elicit a tender, possibly even wistful response? "For what it's worth," he said, looking a little distracted, "you did a really crackerjack job."

But before that, before many years later, there was the day after my first night with Eugene. As you might have figured out by now, I'm a big blabbermouth. I told, well, pretty much all my friends about Eugene. Here is what they thought of him.

Libby: "He must have been the one I saw preening in the hall outside your room. Do you have the word 'twit' in America?"

Obax: "He sounds dreamy. When can you two double-date with Etienne and me?"

Etienne: "Philosophy, it is I am not agreeable with. To find out meaning of the life is for some bourgeois. It is unmeaning."

Anna: "He's a philosopher? Does that mean he's good at life or bad at life?"

Nora: "It doesn't matter what I think of him. Or what you think of him. Boyfriends have short shelf lives."

Paul: "He got you in the sack by using a word you never heard of?! I have to try that one."

George: "Why don't broads ever go for English blokes?"

Evie: "As long as he's not from here, you're fine. Englishmen's teeth are rank."

Norma: "Eugene Obello? Isn't an obello the mark they put in ancient manuscripts to indicate a spurious passage?"

Bronson: "I'm fairly certain an obello was the name of the machete they use in the Philippines."

Not the unanimous endorsement I'd been hoping for.

Nevertheless. Eugene and I started to see each other on a regular basis. It was now typical for me to bicycle over to his place after dinner three or four nights a week, have a glass of wine with him, then proceed to his bedroom until it was time for him to go to sleep. Eugene was strict about racking up seven and a half hours and my presence appeared to interfere with his goal. The one full night I did spend with him gave me insight into what it would be like to share a bed with the Gestapo. Every move I made, however infinitesimal, was subject to interrogation.

Even so, to me, we were dating. I have come to believe, however, that Eugene had a different point of view.

"I don't get it," Libby said one night. It was about one in the morning and we were in her room, engrossed in spirited discourse about ourselves. Also, we were putting nail polish on our toes. I had just returned from Eugene's.

"Surely you don't mean to suggest you *fancy* him?" Libby said, kicking around her feet so the polish would dry faster. Do you hate it as much as I do when the English begin a sentence with the phrase "Surely you don't mean to suggest"? Because, of course, that is exactly what you were going to suggest.

"For one thing," I said, "he's really smart." I held up a bottle of something. "Is this varnish?"

"You Americans," Libby said, "you're all so bloody impressed with a sham Brit accent." She handed me a nail wand. "Use this. It's more expensive."

"Did you know that some people pronounce 'hegemony' with a hard *g*?" I said, deciding to illustrate Eugene's brainpower with an example. "Eugene told me that."

"By the way, everyone we know is smart," Libby said.

"But everyone doesn't say he likes this part of my face," I said, pointing to the part of my face that was below my cheekbone toward my nose.

"We'll see," Libby said. "And Eugene is wrong about 'hegemony.' And that color has too much color."

"Why do you have to ruin everything with facts?" I said.

By the time Libby and I were putting the ridge filler on our nails, Eugene, I figured, was in his fourth hour of sleep. "Define 'deviant,' " I said to Libby, who had just used that word to describe my relationship with Eugene.

"Don't you think that two people who regularly take their clothes off in front of each other at night," Libby said, "should also do stuff together during the day, for instance, talk?"

"Don't you think you're being awfully conventional?" I said, and then, with as much wisdom and weariness as I could affect, I added: "That's not the way things are in the modern world, Libby." Needless to say, how would I know? But who was this Libby to call me weird? She was seeing a guy who had informed her that if they were to make a serious commitment to each other and if she had to have her arm amputated afterward, he would leave her. He wanted her to be aware of that in advance, he said, so she couldn't turn around and blame him later and say he was a bad guy.

Despite what Libby said, Eugene and I did see each other during the day, albeit only on rare occasions. Once I attended a lecture he delivered, "The Fallacy of Fallacies Is a Fallacy." Another time, we met for coffee at the university library. We had a big laugh that day, I recall, about a very old man we saw, we're talking a million years old, who, when told by the librarian that the periodical he'd requested from the stacks would require three to six months to locate, leaned his elbow on the table and said he'd wait. It doesn't seem funny now and, come to think of it, probably wasn't funny then, but what can you do when love is first in flower?

Hold on. It just came to me: something else happened that day at the library. A fragile-looking girl, about my age, fainted by the bicycle rack as we were unlocking our bicycles. I think you would have been as impressed as I was to see how adroitly and gently Eugene helped her up. When she seemed to falter, I

watched Eugene offer her his arm. It almost brought tears to my
eyes. My hero, I thought, though I guess you could say, strictly
speaking, he was her hero. Eugene walked the girl home.

"Good-bye, Genie," I said.

"Ta-ta, my duchess," Eugene said.

I bet you are as down on Eugene as Libby was. I bet you are
thinking: This guy better at least be one hell of a looker. I
already told you I don't describe people. I'm against description.
I will tell you, if you insist, that Eugene had the wire-rimmed
glasses and hollow cheeks of a young Bolshevik during the
Russian Revolution, the organized hair of a boy having his
school picture taken, and the lankiness of a tennis player—but
honestly, none of that matters. I will tell you something that
possibly does matter, something you might remember: Eugene's
eyes were run-of-the-mill, but what he did with them was not.
He had a gaze that made the object of his attention feel, not just
beloved, but absolutely worthy of that love. Of course, he wasn't
looking at you, so maybe you don't care.

I sense I haven't convinced you yet. You know what I think
it really was? He was a narcissist. I love narcissists—even more
than they love themselves. You don't have to buoy them up.
They are their own razzle-dazzle show and you are the blessed,
favored with a front-row seat.

Here's an example. It is not long after I'd met Eugene. He
and I are drinking champagne on top of Castle Hill, which, to
be topographically truthful, should be called Castle Bump. We
are a-flush in celebration because an exalted academic journal
has just accepted Eugene's paper on . . . let me see if I can get
this straight . . . how the thirty-seventh digit of pi is the key to
understanding not just pi but much more, maybe even every-

thing. (Please don't ask me to go into more technical detail about pi than this.)

"Here's hoping that your paper will forever change the way pi is thought of!" I say.

"It will, my juju, it will," he says with pronounced conviction and I believe him. Eugene kisses me—a lot of his body touches a lot of my body—and the next thing I know, he is lecturing me about Isaac Newton and gravity. Just think, I thought: Not far from the dirt mound on which I am having my most titillating moment to date, Sir Isaac Newton, it seems, had formulated his famous law explaining the mutual attraction of objects. I attached a meaning to Newton's discovery, particularly to his universal gravitational constant, that I don't think Newton had intended.

"And that is why," Eugene says, lifting his glass, "he is the greatest scientist of all time." We drink to Isaac Newton or to Eugene or to both, and as we do, the sun sets. Eugene blocks my view.

But that isn't it entirely. It wasn't only Eugene's narcissism that made me fall for him. Name one other guy who ever told me I looked like a French actress?

Afterward I bicycled home on cloud nine. I could hear "Oh, What a Night" blasting from King's Cave, a dance club in the cellar of my college, and I took it personally.

Later that same night, I think it was, Etienne, the boyfriend of my neighbor Obax, stopped by Libby's room, where I had been propounding to her my theory that Stephen Hawking was faking it. "Could it be possible for you to give me the loan of your racket of tennis?" Etienne said.

I can't resist telling you now how much I detested Etienne. He and Obax were polar studies majors. His area was ice thickness; Obax didn't have an area. She thought Etienne was cute and he was—in a Peugeot bicycle kind of way. You'd think that I, of all people, would have been sympathetic to someone enthralled with a guy who nobody considered enthrall-worthy. You'd think, but you'd be wrong.

Soon after Obax met Etienne, she told me she had called her father in Somalia and said, "Daddy, I met the greatest guy and he has a dishwasher!"

"Obax," she said her father had said, "if you are dating a man because he has a dishwasher, I will fly to England and buy you one."

Obax did not tell her father that Etienne was militant about having sex with her three times a day. I don't know if you regard that as a good thing or a bad thing, but I know which side Obax's father would have been on.

Thanks to Etienne, I was morally opposed to marriage. He had told Obax that the institution was *"for seulement le petit bourgeoisie."* That sounded so smart I repeated it for years. For similar reasons, he was also against train schedules—"just because it is when they go, it is when I go?"

It is surprising, then, that it was Etienne who had convinced me to invite Eugene to a May Ball. May Balls, if you don't already know, are extravagant proms held during a week in June. It is a week of drinking and parties and drinking and parties and drinking and parties, followed by drinks. Rumor had it that one of the May Balls was going to feature an open butter bar where dairy lovers could sample various international butters and butter spreads. One might surmise that Etienne would be against such fanfare on the grounds it was for the haute bourgeois; but I guess since Obax had roped him into going, he felt everyone should suffer.

Thus, I found myself one morning, knocking on Eugene's door, intending to ask him to one of the more fab May Balls, whose highlight was slated to be a Jacuzzi filled with "all the champagne you can sit in." When Eugene didn't answer his door or his telephone three days in a row, I asked the porter if he had any news of him. The porter told me that Eugene had left the country.

How could this be? I had seen Eugene not more than a few nights earlier. He had called me his "terra firma." I realize this was not an insurance policy, but . . . how could this be?

I was in anguish.

A week later, I received an international postcard from Eugene. He wrote: "Most dearest, Pop-Pop suffered cardiac arrest. 'Tis a gloomy time. Am in St. Louis—but my heart is with you, my ever-new enchantment."

Never had I been so relieved to hear of a heart stopping. Eugene's grandfather was a famous MIT economist who, according to Eugene, many people say should have gotten the Nobel prize for his work on an economic model that, I swear to God, made possible the express line at the supermarket. Eugene worshiped his grandfather. He needed to be with him. That didn't just make sense to me; I found it touching. And so I would go off for summer break without saying good-bye to Eugene, but I had faith. Eugene's grandfather would recover and so would I.

The next time Eugene disappeared, though, there was not such a happy ending.

At least not for me.

THREE

You're probably going to be bored with anything I say about weather, but I just have to tell you that the night I returned to England from my summer holiday in Philadelphia, the temperature outside was my favorite temperature—room temperature. I had been thinking this as I waited for a taxi outside the Cambridge train station, noticing happily that I could wear a sweater or not wear a sweater and be equally comfortable. It doesn't take much to make me happy. I had still been thinking this when I saw a headline in the copy of the Cambridge *Evening News* that the man standing in front of me was reading. The headline said: HEAT WAVE CONTINUES! TEMP HITS 23! That was Centigrade, of course, but even in Fahrenheit numbers (about 73), I think you get the point.

I forgot to ask: When was the last time you heard the words "holiday" and "Philadelphia" in the same sentence?

It had not been a long holiday. I had intended to loaf around in America for most of the summer, but had gotten a letter from Eugene, my first ever, saying, "My little lamb gone astray—

come back forthwith. Without you, Cambridge is only a topos. Missing you, your Eugene."

Not exactly a love letter; more like a love postcard. But that's all it took. My imagination was off and running: Eugene, poor thing, was languishing in a bleak atelier, eating barely at all, scratching days off on a calendar in anticipation of my arrival. The atelier had no electricity or water, that's how much Eugene was in love. To tell you the truth, if things had been less bleak in my own atelier, I might not have been so galvanized by Eugene's words. I might never have even been galvanized by Eugene in the first place. But that's speculation, and isn't speculation just too speculative?

"I must to England tonight," I announced to my parents, "I need to get back." I wondered if they picked up on the Shakespeare reference. You know the one I mean? My parents looked a little blank, so I added, "For research purposes." This was the night before the family was to drive to Williamsburg in order that my mother might choose a colonial paint color for the living room.

"Baloney," my father said. Speaking as a layman, the man had a point. For starters, I hadn't even picked a thesis topic. Then there was the nonrefundable deposit he had paid to secure our reservations at the fancy inn in Virginia.

"I read that a race riot is going to break out," I said, "and it behooves me not to miss it because what if I write my thesis about the relation between racial conflict and the influx of better mutton to Great Britain?" I didn't even know what I was talking about. My father gave me that look. "Surely," I said, "you wouldn't be the kind of parent who would ask of his child that she pass up a research opportunity of such moment?"

"I do not want my daughter going to a riot," my father said in the tone that he had once said, "You can have dessert without taking two bites of your broccoli when you're grown-up and living in your own house."

"Not a real race riot," I said. "Just the teensiest bit of ethnic tension."

My father looked unconvinced.

"Are you familiar," I said, "with the book *The Logic of Scientific Discovery* by Karl Popper?" Unfortunately, my father was, so I could go no further with my argument since I hadn't read the book.

"Oh, come on, Daddy," I said. "Please, please, please, please, pleeeeeeeeez."

For public record, I'd like to insert here that my father—and my mother, too—were jubilant (at least in theory) to have a daughter in graduate school abroad. That I was studying in Cambridge was consequently a piece of information pressed upon any and all who chanced upon my father during those years. Or so say people I know who witnessed scenes such as this:

Stranger: "Nice weather we're having."

My Father: "Yes, here it is, but in England, it's been raining for a week. At least that's what my daughter says."

Stranger: "How about that."

My Father: "Yes, she's at Cambridge University. In England."

Stranger: "You don't say."

My Father: "She's studying social and political science."

Stranger: "Well, nice talking to you."

My Father: "On a fellowship."

Stranger: "Okay, then. Ohkayyy."

My Father: "Did you know that John Maynard Keynes studied at Cambridge?"

Back to the drama at hand: A muddy green color was selected for the living room and the next day, I flew to England. My father need not have worried about my going to a riot, for as soon as I returned to Cambridge, I plunged myself into aggressively not doing research, let alone anything at all productive. Or do you count self-destruction as productive?

So as not to seem overeager, I waited one, two, three seconds before showing up at Eugene's rooms to proclaim my arrival. Eugene was not there. In an effort to make it look as if the note I pushed under his door was tossed off, I went through seven drafts. And, as you may know, when expressing affection toward someone whose feelings for you have not yet been absolutely defined, it's best to use French. I signed off: *"Plus de Amour et see vous soon. Ciao."*

There was no word of Eugene the next day or the next day or the next day. "Oh, sweetie," Libby said, when I came crying to her late that night. "Do try to be cheery. We haven't yet ruled out the possibility that Genie's grandfather has had another cardiac arrest. Care for a lager?"

With the time difference working for me, I called Eugene's parents in St. Louis as Libby had advised. Eugene's mother didn't know where Eugene was, but she knew that Eugene's grandfather was at a conference in Taipei whose subject matter was, I think she said, the luck gap in lesser-developed economies.

How could this be? I had it in writing: "My little lamb gone astray—come back forthwith." Doesn't that say to you—it does to me—that Eugene wanted him and me to be together for the rest of our lives, as perhaps a shepherd and a lamb are? At the very least, you'd think he would be in town when I got there.

One thing just occurred to me: Shepherds don't lead lambs to slaughter, do they? I better look that up.

I'd have been mad at Eugene, but firsthand experience had

taught me to put my feelings on the back burner (gas, electric? who remembers?) until I knew for a fact that the target of my anger did not have a legitimate excuse. Actually, I'm not referring to my own firsthand experience but to Libby's. Once, when a guy she'd been fixed up with, Quig Sand, failed to meet her at the Arts Theatre in time for the performance of *Myrna Loy Goes to Hell,* she and I had composed a scathing note to him that we referred to as the Mr. Sand Goes to Hell Communiqué. Unfortunately, the reason Quig Sand hadn't shown up at the theater was that he'd been hit by a bus. We calculated that at the very moment Libby slipped the note under his door, he was being wheeled into the operating room for what turned out to be a seven-hour operation. So with anger off-limits at least for the time being, I settled for being simply miserable.

Who's kidding whom? I was really mad.

In need of a pep talk, I looked out my window to see if Libby was open for business. Her curtains were at half-mast and the lights were off, which meant she had a hangover and wanted to be left alone. You see, at this particular moment, life wasn't exactly hunky-dory for Libby, either.

Let's see, where to start . . . Remember Laurence Hesseltine? The timid fellow who used to trail after Libby without speaking? One morning—this was back in March—Libby had found a note slipped under her door. It was from Laurence, and in Latin, it said, "Would one accompany me to the May Ball?" This was the same May Ball that I had not gone to with Eugene. Libby said yes. She believed in taking the first offer. Besides, she was very kind. And she knew Latin.

According to Libby, there was nothing to write home about that night until she and Laurence were getting their picture taken with some of the midgets from Oz—the theme was "Under the Rainbow." It was then, she said, that she had unwittingly made eye contact with him. As Libby found out later, this glance was a signal to Laurence that she was not only in love with him, but that they were practically betrothed. Laurence may have been virtually a mute, but he had a nuanced lexicon of physical gestures.

For the next few days, I would see Laurence standing outside Libby's door for hours on end. He stood there, unwavering, even during the comings and goings of the elegant Neville Shack, Libby's then-beau, whose vocabulary consisted of the words "Let's!" "Do!" and "Must!" On one rare morning when neither Neville nor Laurence was in the vicinity, Libby and I snuck out to a bakery down the street to strategize over muffins about what to do with Laurence. "I believe he wants to shag me," Libby said. "The merciful thing to do is for me to jump him."

Later that day: Libby said that all was copacetic until she unbuckled his belt. There was a painful interval, Libby said, during which Laurence's face metamorphosed into that of someone who has just watched his house swept away by a tornado, his family massacred, his dog poisoned, his favorite pair of pants shrunk in the washing machine, his expensive toupee eaten by the vacuum cleaner, his brand-new car totaled by a truck in a parking accident, his files obliterated by a computer virus, his mortgage application denied by a doltish clerk, his village devastated by the plague, and his beard messed up by a bad barber— and then he recomposed himself, all the while not making any sound. According to Libby, Laurence stood up slowly, hanging on to a pillow that had been on the bed. He looked down. "Whereof one cannot speak," she said he said, "thereof one must be silent." Then he walked slowly out of the room, taking the pillow and leaving his shirt, which he never came back to retrieve.

Looking back, I'd have to say that Libby was wrong to have inferred that Laurence wanted to shag her.

Libby never saw Laurence again. In fact, we don't know any-one who did. After her incident with Laurence, Libby got in touch with Stephen Hawking's people, who said Laurence had left Hawking's house without giving reason. The little old lady in charge of arranging the cosmologist's travel told Libby that she believed Laurence was unstable. We didn't need a little old lady to tell us that.

What we did need was someone to tell us what Laurence meant by "Whereof one cannot speak, thereof one must be silent." It was Eugene (doesn't it figure?) who later told me that the quote was from Wittgenstein, but knowing that still doesn't shed much light on Laurence's behavior. Libby's and my theory was that Laurence must have been flitty, but isn't that always just a default explanation?

Here's the odd part. I mean, here's another odd part. After Laurence disappeared, Libby fell in love with him. If her story were a movie, the poster would say THE LOVE AFFAIR THAT DIDN'T START UNTIL IT WAS OVER!

Libby, whom I had never known to be fazed by any of the numerous admirers who graced her bed, was so distracted by this phantom paramour that she handed in her paper about the role of rudder shields in the Viking navy a week late.

At least there was this: It's always gratifying to share a hobby with a friend, and pining for erstwhile suitors falls into that cat-egory. In the months to come, Libby and I would analyze our respective exes with the gusto and intellectual rigor of Jesuits.

And now, is it okay with you if I get back to me?

Weeks after Eugene disappeared (and what is it about guys that they can't stay put?), a letter came with a postmark I did not recognize. The letter was written on blue paper so gauzy that the diet iced tea I spilled on it obliterated a serious region of the text. "Precious petal," the letter began, "I am sitting on a beautiful white sand beach in Dubrovnik, yearning to be back in Cambridge, sipping tea with you."

That's when I spilled the diet iced tea.

"I'd like to explain how I got here," Eugene wrote, "but, my dear, I'm not sure myself. As fate would have it, a woman I scarcely knew at all rang me up Friday last and asked me to join her in Yugoslavia. She is doing fieldwork in an idyllic hamlet on the Adriatic."

Scarcely knew at all! It's funny, isn't it, how a detail included as a reassuring fact can have the opposite effect.

The letter went on. "I left straightaway. And whilst my feelings for her are an inchoate olio, as yet too jumbled to sort out, my feelings for you are steadfast. Trust, therefore, that these are confounding times for me. At the moment, for example, I feel a little lonesome as she is away for the day, doing some research for a paper she might write involving the oral traditions of various tribes vis-à-vis the passing down of indigenous recipes."

Excuse me for my nervous interrupting, but need I highlight how similar this was to the pretend thesis topic of a certain someone about the relation between racial tension and the influx of better cuts of meat to Great Britain?

In the middle of the letter, there was some stuff about Yugoslavia, in which Eugene explained why the various factions in the country would always live in peace. And then, revisiting the matter of himself and the girl he scarcely knew, he wrote: "I do feel emotionally bound up with her. Indeed, there is some possibility that our relationship may become significant and I thought you ought to know about it."

The next part of the letter was indecipherable because of the tea damage, but I could make out the words "sunburn" and

"sheep yogurt" and "entelechy" and, at the close, "Until we are
'Ich an Du,' Your most indulgent, Eugene."

I was in too much of a state to wonder about it then, but
now I am wondering: Which particular grain of sand on the
beautiful beach in Dubrovnik was the one that ended for me
and began for Margaret a life with Eugene? Or was it a dune?

Margaret was the fragile-looking girl who had fainted by the
bicycle racks outside the library last spring. Remember how
impressed I had been with Eugene for chivalrously volunteering to escort her home safely? What I did not find out until
later from—oh, let's just say I have my ways—was that they had
met some time before the fainting incident while sitting next to
each other at a dinner to which Margaret had been invited by
her tutor, a fellow in Hellenistic studies.

Libby was madder than I was. She promised me fifty pounds
if I would admit that Eugene was a crud. I turned down the
offer. I'm not saying there weren't times I wanted Eugene dead,
but that was because I loved him. To picture him dead was easier and more convenient than picturing him happy with someone else. And I guess I couldn't stop picturing him.

I once read in a magazine that one way to determine whether
you are in love is to ask yourself if you could tolerate the suffering of the person in question. By that definition, I definitely
didn't love Eugene. Still, dead or alive, I always would have taken
him back, to the extent I ever had him in the first place.

I was going to say I hated Margaret, but then, I hate to say,
I remembered I liked her. On the few occasions I was in her
presence, she seemed very decent. Let me give you an exam-
ple. Not too long after Eugene and Margaret came back from
Dubrovnik, I had gone to hear a debate on the proposition
"This House Has No Confidence in the Power of Words to
Sway Public Opinion."

Margaret was there, wearing a pale blue velour top and black jeans. I'd never considered that color scheme before and I have to tell you I was impressed with Margaret's style. She looked wispy and flushed, which is also a smart combination, in my book. As the debate began, I saw Margaret notice me and wave. Margaret was never particularly animated, but she usually did have a smile on her face—something I could never be accused of. It's not that I wouldn't like to have a smile on my face; my face just won't cooperate. Can you see how this warmth of Margaret's could make me more than a little qualmish?

The debate managed to be simultaneously silly and boring. The real drama took place in the audience and concerned a distinguished elderly man wearing an academic gown. He was sitting in front of Margaret so I saw him right away. I also saw right away that he was drinking heartily and with no attempt at disguise from a bottle in a brown bag. In no time, the man started heckling the debaters. "I think Truman," he stood up and yelled, "I think Truman was . . . I think Truman was a . . ." The man wobbled. "You know what I think Truman was?" This was England, so everyone pretended that the man did not exist. He turned around and repeated his question. "Do you know what Harry Truman was?" The debaters carried on as if nothing out of the ordinary was happening and in the audience, people stared ahead with such intensity you'd have thought Sarah Bernhardt was onstage doing *Phaedra*. "Harry Truman," the man pointed his finger, "was a *jolly good egg*." The man lurched toward the stage.

"Surely you do not have the temerity to suggest," said one of the debaters to the other as the drunken man jumped onto the stage, "that a metaphor or a simile or even a participial flair has the staying power punch of an AK-47?"

The drunken man was now standing a few inches from one

of the debaters. "Be vewwy vewwy quiet," he said in a stage whisper. "I'm hunting wabbits!"

Very calmly and with great authority, Margaret made her way up to the stage and escorted the man out of the room. I don't know what she did after that, but her performance in the auditorium was stunning. Margaret may look neurasthenic, but she's a doer.

The only thing I had against Margaret other than her existence is that she wrote her thesis about shoe imagery in Homer. You might even have seen her thesis because a few years ago, an academic press published it as a monograph. It was called "Achilles' Heel and Athena's Sandal: Shoe Imagery in Homer." This really got to me because, as anyone who knows me will tell you, I am the shoe expert.

At any rate, one morning, a few days after I'd gotten Eugene's letter, he showed up. He was wearing a loose-fitting linen shirt, I suspect from Yugoslavia. Before he said anything, he hugged me in the overlong way a person hugs someone, say, whose father or mother has recently died. What I felt was deep embarrassment.

Eugene was still hugging me when Obax from next door walked in. "I'm going to Boots," Obax said. She seemed not to notice Eugene. "Need anything?"

Obax and I loved Boots Chemist, especially their clip-on barrettes and their painkillers. Eugene disengaged himself from me and sat on the veal-colored chair, which perfectly complemented his suntan. I leaned against my desk.

I asked Obax what she was buying at Boots. She wasn't getting anything. She pointed in the direction of her room.

"Yikes," I said. Etienne had become extremely possessive of Obax. He was so hard to get rid of, we'd nicknamed him Rash. For the last few days, Etienne had been camping out in Obax's room so he could keep her in check. If you thought it was bad when Etienne required that Obax do it with him three times a day, what do you think about four times? Errands were her only reprieve. Libby and I had urged Obax to get rid of Etienne, but why should she be the only sane one in this story?

"You've been on my mind," Eugene said as soon as Obax left. He furrowed his brow, either to demonstrate that I'd been on his mind or to express his condolences. "How *are* you?"

"Good," I said, lest he think otherwise. "How about you?"

"If you want to know the truth," he said, and needless to say, one never does want to know the truth, "it's been a complicated interim." Eugene sighed. "On the one hand, I have developed quite tender feelings for Margaret in the short amount of time I have known her. On the other hand, I have feelings for you as well. It's all so thorny." Eugene held up his hands to indicate how trying the situation was for him. I scrunched my nose, so as to look supportive. "I am well aware that any decision will bring pleasures and regrets," he said. Pleasures and regrets for him, I was pretty sure he meant. I was also pretty sure his decision would bring mostly pleasures for him. I nodded.

"So, if you can find it in your heart . . ." I nodded again. "I suppose what I would like you to do, my seraph of reason," Eugene said, "is sit tight." He stood up and walked to the door. He stopped. "Well," he said. I took that as a sign that it was my turn to talk.

Be a good sport, be a good sport, be a good sport, I thought. "It occurs to me," I said, "that your birthday is coming up." Eugene smiled. "Why don't you and Margaret come over and I'll cook you both dinner?"

Eugene looked perplexed.

"What? We have a kitchen on the floor," I said.

He hesitated. "That would be lovely," he finally said and then he seemed not to know what else to say. I wasn't overflowing with subject matter, either. We looked at each other. We looked away. We looked at each other. We looked away. This went on for a while, or that is how I understood it from my end. Then Etienne barged in.

"Do you know where is l'O? She is to be typing my paper about the ice disasters that the Danes did. I was out and so, when I reenter to see what is up with the what, she leaves a writing she is at the Boots Chemist."

"That's where she is, Etienne," I said.

Etienne snarled and left.

Eugene hugged me again as if this time my whole family had perished, probably in a mudslide. And then it popped into my head that the problem with him and me was that I had not been nice enough. My callous disposition must have driven Eugene to Margaret. I had not, for instance, ever told Eugene in all the time we'd known each other how I felt about him. My policy with Eugene and everyone else was: Never go out on a limb unless you are following someone out there. I was a "me, too" girl. "I missed you." *"I missed you, too."* "I love you." *"Me, too, you."* "Do you want to spend the night?" *"If you want me to."* But now I told myself: Show some guts. Take a stand. Be a man.

I took a deep breath. "You know," I said, looking down, "I really like you." Actually, by the time I got to the end of my sentence what came out was, "Ahrellehlicku."

Eugene put his hand on my shoulder and looked straight into my eyes with unnerving commiseration. "I know you do," he said.

That was it. The Like of My Life. Never again, I vowed silently, would I disclose my affections. If I liked someone, I would keep it to myself. To be really on the safe side, I would never even confess to knowing the person.

Eugene looked at his watch. "I should be going," he said.

"Me, too," I said. "I mean, okay, bye."

"Wait," said Eugene. "I'd like to linger." He took his hand off the doorknob and looked at his watch again. This time he tried to be inconspicuous about it, though I noticed, so where was the inconspicuity? "But I'm meeting up with Margaret at the Grad Pad," he said. "We're taking lunch at the new wine bar in Grantchester. Have you tried it yet?"

"I hear it's good," I said, with fake good nature.

"I'm glad you're taking this so well, my sweet sport," said Eugene. "The last thing I want to do is hurt you." That was the last thing he did, but I wasn't going to be the one to break it to him. Still, it upset me to see him so rapidly switch from solemn to jaunty.

Do you want to know how my friends weighed in at this point?

Obax: "How clever to invite Eugene and Margaret to dinner. Promise me you'll use my recipe for crabmeat fricassee."

Libby: "You know how everyone is always saying go with your heart, trust your instinct, have the courage of your convictions? My advice to you is not to listen to those people."

Anna: "This raises a crucial question: Would it be more loathsome were Eugene lying or telling the truth? Never mind. The answer just came to me."

Nora: "Stop right there. He went to Dubrovnik and didn't bring you back a piece of hand-painted ceramic?"

Paul: "Say what you want, I think it was genteel of him to stop by and be square with you."

George: "On the one hand, he's a cad. On the other hand, I wish I could trade places with him."

Evie: "It's his shirt that distresses me most. It wasn't like a muumuu, was it?"

David: "Next time you see Eugene, ask him what he thought of the new offering of late-harvest wines in Grant-chester."

Bronson: "I guarantee you will never see that man again."

Here's an amazement. Eugene took me up on my invitation to have him and Margaret for dinner. They came on the very night of his birthday, which I, in my hopeless optimism, interpreted as proof that Eugene was not getting along with Margaret. If it had been love, wouldn't they have spent the night in a more romantic way? I was also encouraged because Margaret was wearing green with brown, usually an interesting choice, but her green was too kelly. I was wearing pale blue with black, which I had previously deduced he liked.

My hopeless optimism did not last long. Anarchists had blown up a British admiral a couple of weeks earlier while he'd been boating in Ireland. During our conversation about that, I was perfectly cheerful. Ditto our discussion about the so-called Butcher on the Moors, who had just been suspected of killing a twelfth victim after the body of a woman was discovered in an alleyway. I was riding high through that, too. In the middle of our chat about the spacecraft that had fallen out of the sky, though, Margaret had said offhandedly, "Gene bean, didn't your mother say that a piece had landed near their cottage when we were visiting last month?" I don't need to tell you how many ways that deranged me. Whether Eugene realized that Margaret had just belied his claim that they had hardly known each other when she had invited him to Dubrovnik, I don't know. You couldn't tell by the way he continued to chuck back the wine.

"Does this have gluten?" Margaret asked about the birthday cake. Margaret had a gluten allergy—isn't that perfect? Even if

I had known the difference between gluten and nongluten flour, I couldn't have answered the question for I had not made the cake I was pretending to have made. It had been left over from a dinner party that Obax had had the night before—she'd made two different kinds as an experiment in frosting. I chose my words about the gluten carefully. "Not exactly," I said. It's not that I would have minded killing Margaret; I just didn't want to get blamed. "Not exactly," I felt confident, could legally be yes or no.

After dessert, Margaret and Eugene exchanged a look that said, I can't stand this one second longer, let's scram! "We should go," said Eugene. "Yes," said Margaret, adding, I swear, "I have a lot of Petrarch to get through tonight."

The next morning, Libby came over very early. I hadn't even arranged the curtains to indicate I was accepting visitors. "They had as bad a time as I did, so that's something," I said. I was about to recount every detail of the night when the horror-struck expression I noticed on her face stopped me.

She was holding a piece of paper. "You'll never believe this," she said. "I got a note from Laurence Hesseltine's father. Laurence hanged himself."

"You're kidding?" I said, stunned.

"I'm funny, but I'm not that funny," said Libby, but not in a funny way. "Listen," she said and began reading from the note. " 'As Laurence friend, please know beloved son found hanged Bradford. Funeral facts anon. Cause unknown. Mr. J.G.H., Esq.' "

We stood silent for a long time. We both had a theory about the cause—the same theory.

We stood silent some more.

"I'm fairly certain Bradford is where they found the body of the woman they think was murdered by the Butcher on the Moors," Libby said.

"Wait," I said. "You think there's a connection between Laurence and the Butcher on the Moors?"

"No," Libby said. "No, I don't. I was just thinking."

We stood for a long time more. I was thinking about how he had died a virgin and I wondered if that was a sad thing or a happy thing for a human being, even Laurence.

The good news was that the gravediggers' strike had ended in Laurence's hometown. And that the heat wave had broken.

FOUR

L̲ibby and I did not go to Laurence's funeral. Worse, neither of us had sent a condolence note to Mr. and Mrs. Hesseltine. It's one of those things I'll always feel lousy about. But how could we tell his parents we were sorry? What if they had then said, "Oh, *now* you're sorry?" Or what if we had said we were sorry exactly at the moment they had clean forgotten their only child had done away with himself? The last thing Libby and I wanted to do was stir things up and make the Hesseltines sad all over again.

Of course, the real reason was this: Wouldn't saying we were sorry sound like an apology? Wouldn't they conclude that we'd done it? Partly, we had. That was the problem. Don't forget, I had been in on Libby's decision to . . . I'd rather not use the word "rape" here, but you know what I mean.

We didn't know then what I know now: that expressing sympathy is like a pass-fail exam. You get credit merely for making the effort. In our defense, this was the first nonpet death either of us had ever had to deal with.

The day after the telegram came from Laurence's father,

Eugene stopped by. I'm still not sure whether his real purpose had been to thank me for dinner (unlikely), tell me his grandfather had died (perhaps), or pick up the jacket he'd left in my room (where I'm laying my bet). In any case, he stayed only a few minutes because he had to catch a plane to St. Louis for the funeral.

Eugene welled up. "Did I tell you that I will be giving a eulogy along with a Nobel prize winner, the deputy secretary of agriculture under Eisenhower, and the public advocate for Cincinnati?" he said.

"Isn't that something?" I said.

"The obituary consultant we hired was so impressed with Pop-Pop's accomplishments," Eugene said, "that he told me he wished my grandfather hadn't died." That thought seemed to cheer up Eugene. He smiled. "I wish you could have met him," he said.

Maybe I had looked confused. "My grandfather," Eugene said. Eugene gave me one of his hugs. "I should go. I have to be at the airport by three." He walked toward the door, then stopped and turned. "This talk has really meant a lot to me."

I was dying to ask whether Margaret was going to the funeral. Instead, I said I was sorry.

"I know you are," he said.

Eugene's Pop-Pop had stayed dead, but Libby had bounced back. Soon after we didn't go to Laurence's funeral, she became stage manager at the Amateur Dramatic Club. During a production of Sheridan's *The Rivals,* Libby took up with the guy who was playing the part of Lydia Languish. Libby found him amiable enough company even though, according to a reviewer for the *Varsity,* "he did not pout in quite the correct eighteenth-century manner."

That made two of us who had gotten over Laurence's death with a sort of shameful dispatch, but I had most decidedly not gotten over Eugene. I especially had not gotten over the apparent ease with which he had gotten over me. Or was it that in Eugene's mind, there had been nothing to get over? When you are the person who cares, don't you find it inconceivable that the person you care about couldn't care less? Unfortunately, the clearer it became that Eugene was not in love with me, the more convinced I became that he and I could have been just the thing. How could I ever expect to meet someone as wonderful as Eugene?

Besides, the prospect of getting to know someone again seemed as wearisome as filling out a form: "Do you have any brothers or sisters?" "Do you like Thai food?" "Yes, I could live in Paris, too." "Have you ever torn a ligament?" "You're left-handed? How fascinating! When's your birthday? Would you rather burn or freeze to death?" Of course, Eugene never asked me those questions and vice versa, but he was Eugene.

So Eugene had dropped by for five minutes, said cheerio (really), and I was a wreck for weeks. I devoted every hour, it seemed, to diet iced tea—getting it and drinking it. As far as I knew, and this was an area I had come to have an embarrassing expertise in, the only place in Cambridgeshire that sold the drink was Babbington Brothers and Danks Vintners, an establishment primarily known for being the first in town to carry Nouveau Beaujolais each Nouveau Beaujolais season. (*LE NOUVEAU NOUVEAU BEAUJOLAIS EST ARRIVE!!!!!* proclaimed their banner, as if they were announcing the coming of Christ or a really great clothes sale.) The bicycle ride to and from the vintners took something along the lines of forty-five minutes; I could manage twelve bottles per trip; it took me approximately an hour and a half to drink my haul. Can you see how this could become a maniacal pursuit?

Incidentally, I was the Babbington Brothers and Danks's only customer when it came to bottles of diet iced tea. After I left Cambridge forever, I pictured the soda distributor in East Anglia scratching his head, trying to comprehend why sales of diet iced tea had spiked to phenomenal numbers, remained consistently strong for a year, then dropped precipitously.

It was Obax who'd finally lifted me out of my funk, coincidentally at around the same time she was descending into hers. At a fund-raiser hosted by the Friends of the Scott Polar Research Institute, Obax had put it together that Etienne was having an affair with Sybil Sawtell. Have you heard of the Sawtells? They own all the water in the South Pole—or is it the North Pole? Sybil, or as Obax called her, "Sybil of Liquid Wealth," was a Friend. To give you an idea of her sophistication, let me tell you what Obax said Etienne said Sybil said before she went off to Paris for the weekend: "Is the Louvre worth going to?"

Obax figured out that Sybil of Liquid Wealth was more than a Friend to Etienne when Obax saw Etienne put his hand under Sybil's jumper by the punch bowl. Etienne and Sybil were deep in an embrace at the time.

Guess what Etienne said when Obax confronted him after the fund-raiser? "You do not care about me certainly if you never know until now about Sybil and me. Sibby and I are an attractive unit for a longest time and if you truly loved me you would noticed I liked her before this now." No matter how desperately Obax pleaded, Etienne refused to give up Sybil of Liquid Wealth. "I wanted to speak with someone I could not identify with and that is my Sib. She has not to do with you and the problems of you," Etienne said. Etienne wished—and his wish was always his command—to continue to live with Obax and see Sybil on the side. "That is to be French," Etienne said, as if it were a good thing.

Obax wept for days. Etienne found her tears so irksome, he

gave her sedatives. Whether she took the tablets because she was miserable or whether it was the other way around, I don't know. The astonishing part was that Obax was still nuts about Etienne. But who am I to judge?

Obax lay in Etienne's bed, catatonic, watching the telly until BBC1 went off the air every night with *Badger Watch*. This was a ten-minute segment in which a camera was set up next to a tree while an announcer whispered portentously about whether tonight was going to be the night the badger would finally, dare we even think, come out of his hole.

To Obax's credit, though, she still had the good sense to suggest that it would be therapeutic for me to take the train back and forth from Cambridge to London all day long, day after day. On British Rail, a passenger did not pay per mile, as it were. Rather, you paid only when you got off the train, the rate determined by where you started and where you ended as long as you stayed on the train. This was one of those fantastic deals that not many people were interested in taking advantage of.

I took the 7:42 to King's Cross every morning with the commuters. I didn't step onto the platform at Cambridge again until the 11:30 pulled in at 12:37 with the theatergoers, swingers, hooligans, truants, men who looked like the types who pretended they had had to work late, stragglers who missed the 10:30, and a pervert or two. In the meantime, I sat in my compartment, not paying attention to what was outside—depressed-looking villages and the rare cow, also looking a little down. Nor did I read, because I had a tendency to pack books for the person I wanted to be (say, Karl Popper's *The Logic of Scientific Discovery*), not the person I was (Harrods catalogs and crossword puzzles). I sat, thinking about my lot, and drinking diet iced tea.

One afternoon—call it my twenty-third consecutive afternoon—on the 4:47 to London, as I was staring at a page in a book I would never get to the next page in, I heard the door of my compartment slide open. "Anyone sitting here?" a male voice asked. I was ready with my usual answer, one that never failed to repel potential seat-takers. "Just the Lord!" I said—no, chirped.

"Would have reckoned He'd be in a first-class car, no?" the voice said. I looked up.

Oliver Qas, the guy I hadn't slept with my first night in Cambridge due to virginity, took off his cape with a swish and dropped it onto the seat. I had an I-am-in-a-comedy-from-the-thirties feeling. Accordingly, I braced myself for the strain of trying to be witty. "The Lord's a cheapskate," I said, realizing I was not being witty at all.

Oliver brushed his cape aside and sat down. "A seat for a cigarillo," he said and took out an elegant little package. "Look here," said Oliver, handing me a lit cigarillo, "I'm off to see a play about the Nazis' torture of homosexuals. Why don't you come along? Should be good fun."

"It's tempting," I said, and I meant it, "but I'm going back and forth to London all day." My explanation, I decided, needed further explanation. "To kill time, basically."

Oliver shrugged. "Smashing. I'll do that."

"What about the play?" I said.

"Sounds rather gruesome, don't you think?" he said.

Oliver and I smoked grown-up-looking cigarettes as we ricocheted to London and back all day. I never mastered the mechanics of inhaling, but I did the best I could. When the last train pulled into Cambridge at 12:37, Oliver said, "What time tomorrow?"

And so, for days on end, the two of us rode the train, getting nowhere. They were days of contentment. Sisyphus on a date was the way Oliver put it. "Here's an idea," he said one night as we neared Bishop's Stortford. "I duck out in London, grab a batch of Harrods catalogs and some of those Chinese noodles, then pop on the eight thirty-five and we'll do buffet, what?" I was touched that Oliver was willing to pay two fares.

When Oliver's tutor finally insisted he stay in one place, I stepped off the train for good, too. We spent the next, oh, call it 196 hours together, mostly in his rooms, mostly painting a mural of a still life, though if you'd seen it, that would be the last thing you'd guess. "Here's an idea," Oliver said finally, and he smeared the wall with black. " 'Still Life, Moved.' "

Oliver and I fooled around a bit in a state of semi-undress, though how far we got depends on your definitions. "There's something I ought to tell you," Oliver said one night.

"Yes?" I said.

"I'm bisexual," he said.

"Do you really think that is any business of mine?" I said.

I had a confession, too. "Oliver," I said with import days later. We were in the cheese shop because he had had an epiphany the day before that cheese rinds had zero calories. Based on this calculation, erroneous, as it happened, Oliver and I had decided to go on the cheese rind diet. Many cheese shops give the rinds away free of charge, in case you're interested. "Oliver," I said, "I think you should know that I am still pining for Eugene."

Oliver picked up a shard of Gouda and, with what I thought to be excessive fierceness, began to peel off the wax. "Do you really think," he said, "that is any business of mine?"

I found a piece of sage Derby that didn't have too much mold and gave it to him. He seemed to brighten. "I'm thinking that the whole hostage crisis is bang out of order," said Oliver. If anyone other than Oliver had said this, I would have figured he was referring to something that was going on in the news. Oliver, however, believed the news was too up-to-the-minute to merit attention. "So here's my idea," said Oliver. "A rescue mission."

"This isn't going to involve children or hiking, is it?" I said.

"We must do something about your pal—the one who's so slavishly devoted to the French miscreant," said Oliver. "She's off the trolley."

Which is how Oliver, Libby, and I came to show up at Etienne's on a day we knew he was away in Irkutsk at the Siberian Film Festival. Etienne had moved Obax into his flat, the one with the dishwasher she had once bragged about to her father. Obax sat in the living room all day, supposedly translating Etienne's thesis, which had something to do with the arctic ice thickness anomaly of the 1890s. For dinner, Obax served Etienne food she bought from the pub across the street. This was someone who had routinely made her own horseradish from scratch. They ate on paper napkins so she never even got to use his dishwasher.

When we arrived, Obax had on these ridiculous striped pajamas of Etienne's. If she had been wearing just the tops, it might have looked fetching, but she had on the bottoms, too, and the package was dismal. The morass of papers surrounding her did not bring more cheer to the picture.

"Obax," said Libby, "he's worse than the guy you went out with before Etienne."

I turned to Libby. "The one who stole books?" I said.

"No," said Libby. "The one who used to enter his Banbury cakes at village fetes under the cover of a pseudonym."

I'd forgotten about him. He wore clogs.

Oliver walked over to Obax and kneeled before her. "What is it with you girls, letting these good-for-nothings muck up your lives?" he said to nobody and everybody. Nobody responded. "Obax, can't you understand?" Oliver said.

"I don't care to understand," Obax said. "And Bertram didn't steal books. He erased the price and scribbled in an amount he felt was just."

Libby stood behind Obax and silently mouthed to Oliver and me: "This is futile. I'm going swimming." Libby sidled over to the door. "Anyone for a dip?" Oliver shook his head and grabbed my elbow, so there was no going anywhere for me.

Obax got up slowly. "I'm going to the White Swan to buy Cornish pasties and shepherd's pies. Ta." And that ended that.

Life was otherwise peachy. I loved my new haircut (no point in describing it since you never knew my old haircut). And Oliver helped me pick a thesis topic: "Racism and Immigration in Great Britain from the End of the Second World War to the Present, with Particular Consideration of the West Indians Living in London and How Their Expectations of England Compares with Their Experiences After They Arrived." Oliver had assured me that his father, who was from Trinidad, would be pleased as punch to write my thesis for me.

Oliver's father was off the hook. I slogged away in the library. And it was with pride and relief that I was ready by the spring to submit the product of my drudgery for review. At long, long last! I managed without Oliver's father, but I never could have done it without Oliver.

Then you-know-who breezed into town.

"I was talking to Sean Shanahan," Eugene said over coffee at the Black Kettle, a couple of days after he said he'd arrived in town, which was also a couple of days before I planned to turn in my thesis. "He doesn't believe it's one hundred percent certain that the committee will approve your thesis. He says it's a provocative piece of writing, but perhaps deficient in data." Eugene looked at me with his empathetic eyes. "To be frank, I don't really know what data is—I'm more concerned with the intuitive experience of what presents itself to us in conscious experience—you know, I'm a phenomenologist—but forget me. Whatever data is, I propose you get some."

"You know Sean Shanahan?" I said.

"Any husband of someone who shares with my fiancée a passion for all things Homeric is a friend of mine," Eugene said. I thought he was making a joke. Eugene took a careful little nip from a scone, but even so, jam dribbled down his chin.

My heart sank for too many reasons to recite. "I pray this news not cause you consternation, my tender duckling," he said.

"No, no, no," I said. "No, no, no, no." Here's a tip: Repeating something seven times in a row is probably always a give-away that you mean the opposite. Eugene, however, said, "Those are encouraging words," and then he licked the jam off his bottom lip.

"It's divine to see you," he said. Eugene daintily wiped his mouth with a napkin. "You've dwelt in my thoughts."

This did not have the ring of truth. "How's Margaret?" I said, for the record. Eugene still had jam on his face.

"She caught some sort of bug on the plane," Eugene said, "but thank you for asking." Eugene leaned in to signal he was going to say something confidential, never a good sign. "Between you and me, I think she'd have preferred to stay in the States, but what can you do?" He chuckled. "Her Brit-loving fiancé lucked out with a teaching fellowship in Cambridge."

If I looked how I felt, I looked bad. I dug my fingernails into my knee.

"I didn't tell you we were engaged in St. Louis?" Eugene said.

Wouldn't you just know my parents told me that very night, during our weekly telephone conversation, that they planned to visit?

"This is the worst possible time," I said. "I'll be in London getting some data."

I heard my mother say something about data but there was too much static on the line to make out more than that.

"I'm not some phenomenologist," I said, hoping that might address whatever it was my mother had said.

"We want to see you," my mother said.

"I was just home this summer," I said.

I wonder if, at that moment, Sylvia Plath's letters to her mother ran through my own mother's mind. In particular, the one in which Plath had written: ". . . Oh, Mummy, I am over-joyed at the thought that I will see you soon—but sad that your stay will not last forever. . . . O, to share London with you! And travel, hand in hand, to whatever other parts of the world you'd like to see. . . . I cannot stop crying (with happiness!)."

Still, when all is said and done, letters included, which daughter would you want?

"We'll stay at the Beans'," said my father, "and so will you." Arnie and Polly Bean, old friends of my parents, were living in London for the year so that Arnie could set up a community outreach program for the Lumb hamburger restaurant chain. The company, according to Arnie, "wanted Lumb to be about more than hamburgers."

It was hard to say whom I was mad at the most: Eugene, my parents, or, for having an elegant town house in Knightsbridge with extra bedrooms, the Beans.

"This is a very important juncture in race relations in this country. I don't know if I can afford the time to see you," I said.

"Bring some nice clothes," my mother said.

British race relations were on their own for a while because the next day, I was in a taxi with my parents on our way to the Beans'. It wasn't much of a consolation, but at least I would be staying alone in the carriage house while their housekeeper was on vacation. "I must warn you," I told my parents, in a manner that would lead one to expect fairness to come, "I cannot spend any time during the day with you because I will be in the field, gathering data." Some of that was true—the part about not spending any time with them.

It was also true I had devised a questionnaire that I expected, somehow, to hand out to a significant sample of the West Indian population—assuming, that is, I could figure out how to meet them. Every morning, with a stack of questionnaires in my tote bag, I'd say good-bye to my parents and to the Beans—off to do, you know, research. "Do you generate your own hypotheses?" Polly Bean, who'd been a sociology major at Smith College, said to me during breakfast. With that one exception, nobody ever questioned what it was that I did. What I actually did was visit every food shop in London, looking for Lion's roasted-chicken-flavored crisps.

I better explain. Snooping around the housekeeper's carriage house my first night, I came upon a supply of crisps and ate the entirety, I suppose to get even with Eugene, my parents, the Beans, and also, for kindly allowing me the use of her digs, the Beans' housekeeper. The next day, I'd intended to replace the chips, but at a local supermarket discovered that Lion's had, since the time the Beans' housekeeper had purchased her crisps, revamped their packaging. The roasted-chicken-flavored variety now came in a red bag with a yellow logo and a blue lion instead of the yellow bag with the red logo and the green lion. You're probably thinking, So what? But I was thinking, If I buy the crisps in the new red bag with the new yellow logo and the new blue lion, the housekeeper will go straight to Arnie and Polly Bean and tell them that I not only ate her crisps but, even shoddier, that I had the audacity to try to get away with replacing them with other, newer crisps.

Where was I to find the old crisps? Sensitive to the plight of the underclass, I had a hunch that the almighty capitalist would dump his past-its-expiration-date stock into the poor neighborhoods. And so, every morning I headed out to what I imagined to be the other side of the tracks. In anticipation of the one-in-a-zillion chance that I might run into Eugene, I made sure to wear the chichi coat my mother had bought me the day she arrived.

"Excuse me," I'd say to a Pakistani greengrocer in Waltham Forest, "do you carry Lion's crisps?" He would point to a shelf lined with every kind of crisps Lion's made. I would walk slowly down the aisle, surveying the merchandise as if I were perusing a museum exhibit, determine that there were no stale bags of Lion's, and walk out.

I must have visited every immigrant establishment in London. How sad to think of all the data that was there for the asking had I only had the presence of mind to ask. As for the crisps, I could only hope that the Beans' son, who was staying in the housekeeper's quarters after me, would be blamed.

Have you noticed this about being a foreigner? The instant your parents visit, you are no longer a foreigner. You are thirteen and you are living at home. Let's say you had been sitting next to my parents and me at the premier French restaurant in London. You would have seen me order a side salad and only a side salad, acutely aware that my parents would be charged for a three-course price-fixed meal. "The chef is flexible," the waiter would have said upon my request that there be no lardoons in my salad, "but he is not that flexible."

"In that case," I would have said with forced insouciance, "nothing for me." There are always the rinds on my parents' cheese plate, I would have thought. The waiter would have scowled and I would have said, "Maybe some water."

If you had left London with my parents and me and gone with us on our tour of Decayed Stately Homes with Big Doorknobs and then from there traveled with us to Cambridge, you would have seen a lot of me sulking. You might also have seen my parents and me having dinner in the premier Chinese restaurant in Cambridge. I had invited Libby, and during introductory conversation, you would have seen my mother turn to Libby and say in sincerity—by this time, my mother had been through a lot of restaurant experiences with me, don't forget— "Do you *eat*?" And later you would have seen Libby kick me under the table—well, I guess you wouldn't have seen that, but it happened. The reason Libby kicked me, and this you would have seen, was that the maître d' was escorting a party of two toward us, including the very fellow who had darkened (and lightened) my existence.

Eugene stopped by our table. He was with his friend TB, short for Toby Bubbles. "A pleasure indeed," Eugene said to my parents. "Your daughter never ceases to effuse about you." By this time, you know me well enough to know that Eugene was lying. Nevertheless, my mother promptly invited Eugene and TB to join us. The interpretation I prefer is that she wanted to be surrounded by people who didn't mind a lardoon or two in their salads.

Eugene and TB were celebrating their election to the Cambridge Disciples, a secret society of intellectuals (and during the twenties and thirties, spies) whose members seem eager to tell you anything you want to know about their organization, even if you don't ask.

"I suppose I shouldn't divulge this," TB said, "but the society has had a very homoerotic past."

"I tried hypnosis to quit smoking," my father said, "but it didn't work." The acoustics, not good to begin with, had just been made worse by the children's birthday party now seated at the table next to us.

"*Ho-mo-eee-rotic, honey!*" my mother shouted. A woman I

took to be the mother of the birthday boy looked over at us. The birthday boy giggled.

"Mum's the word," TB said extra loudly as he put his fork and knife down and leaned in over the table, "but Prince Charles sought membership."

"How interesting," my mother said. "Uhn-huh," my father said. Then nobody said anything for a while.

"The chancellor's leg," Libby said. "What does everyone think will happen to it?"

"Pardon me, but there's a limb up for grabs?" TB said.

Libby and I exchanged an incredulous look. TB's field was plant sciences (his specialty: diseased soil), but even so, how could anyone be that out of touch? Weren't daily reports in the *Cambridge News* (albeit in a middle section near the classifieds) updating the condition of the university chancellor's gangrenous leg? It is fair to say it was just about the only thing Libby and I were truly interested in at the time.

"Libby thinks they'll save the leg, but I think they'll have to chop it off," I said. "We bet fifty pounds." I saw the mother of the birthday boy mooch her head toward our table and nod in agreement.

"No," said Libby. "My wager was that thanks to extraordinary medical intervention, he'd keep his leg for five months. Then . . ." Libby made a ripping sound.

"After my grandfather had the heart attack that ultimately took his life," said Eugene, "we thought he might lose a toe." That shut everyone up again. Before the night was over, Eugene managed to get in that his grandfather had been a contender for the Nobel prize. I noticed that even the mother of the birthday boy shed a tear.

In the taxi back to my parents' hotel, my father said, "Eugene's very well spoken."

"I think he likes you," my mother said.

"Is he eligible?" my father said.

The best tack in these situations, I always feel, is to grunt indecisively.

The next morning, my parents returned to London and I ran into Margaret after saying good-bye to them. I was carrying a large shopping bag full of shampoo and conditioner that my mother had brought from Philadelphia because I had been complaining that it was impossible to find decent hair products in Britain. Margaret was on her way to the doctor because her feet itched.

"Eugene told me that your parents are sublime," she said.

It was either to my advantage or disadvantage to agree with Margaret, but I didn't have the time to figure out which. "Yeah, well," I said. "Sublime."

Margaret lifted her foot out of an espadrille and, with ballerina poise, raised it high enough so she could scratch her sole without bending. For someone so frail, Margaret had remarkable balance. "Eugene found the experience of being with your family so moving," she said, "he cried when he came home. You know how Eugene loves family. And I suppose you heard he just lost his grandfather?" I said I was sorry. I wished I hadn't said that, but I couldn't take it back.

As Margaret scratched away, I became aware that one of the bottles of hair conditioner was leaking. I became aware of this because the shopping bag had torn and goop was dripping down my leg. "I think it was seeing the love between you and your parents," said Margaret, "that convinced Eugene he couldn't wait until next year for us to get married."

If Margaret did not stop scratching her foot, I was going to kill her. "Would you like some hair conditioner," I said, "it might help."

Margaret looked confused, then returned to her point. "We're going to have the ceremony next week in King's Chapel. It goes without saying that we'd be honored if you were there."

"Next week . . . next week I'll be doing research," I said. "Otherwise, I wouldn't have missed it for the world."

"What a pity," said Margaret, returning her foot to her espadrille and managing to show off her engagement ring in the process. "But I do understand." My shopping bag disintegrated completely and all the bottles hit the ground.

"Did Eugene mention that he talked to Sean?" Margaret said. I braced myself. "Sean's terribly excited about your thesis but feels you should have actual blacks give out the questionnaires in the West Indian community. Ciao." Margaret hopped off to her doctor's appointment.

And not long after, I solicited the opinions of one and all:

Libby: "You don't think that Margaret has what the chancellor has, do you? I'm going to go out on a limb here—sorry!—and wager that Margaret loses everything below the ankle."

Oliver: "If you move to London as Eugene ordains, then all our meaningless train riding will have had no meaning. Trust me: Data is not your problem."

Anna: "Are you really moving to London? Can I use your pass to the pool?"

Nora: "Let me be blunt. You should never use hair conditioner."

Paul: "I never met Margaret, and I hope you don't take this the wrong way, but is it possible that she just has bigger bristols than you?"

George: "If you need someone else to give out questionnaires, I think I might have had a grandfather who was from Puerto Rico."

Evie: "Lice?"

Norma: "I don't want to give you false hope, but itching can be a sign of organ failure."

Bronson: "I guarantee you that Eugene and Margaret will never get married."

"Out of the question," I said to my mother over the phone when she asked if I could see her and my father again before they left. "The Beans would like to see you, too," my mother said. In light of the crisps affair, I heard this as: "The principal would like to see you in his office right now!"

"Mom, I'm at a crossroad with my data."

The truth was that for the last three days, ever since it had sunk in that Eugene and Margaret were getting married imminently, I hadn't gotten out of my bathrobe. The other truth was that I missed my parents, but that wasn't the kind of thing I went around saying.

My father got on the line. "What's this about being too busy to see us?"

I could have told my parents the gloomy facts. But, come on! How heavy-handed can you be? I chose to say nothing.

"I hope you realize," my father said, "these are the best times of your life." What if he was right?

My parents flew back to Philadelphia the next day.

The good news was that the chancellor's leg was amputated within the month and I won my bet with Libby.

FIVE

$\mathbf{M}$y passport indicates that I spent much of the summer in the United States, but what I did there, I cannot recall. I'm assuming it wasn't worth remembering. I could tell you, naturally, what Eugene was doing (besides not getting in touch with me). According to Sean Shanahan, Eugene and Margaret had taken their honeymoon in a little town in Italy that some scholars refer to as the birthplace of the Age of Reason. They spent the rest of the summer in Princeton because Eugene was teaching a seminar on the unsolved problems in philosophy. I consider Eugene to be the apotheosis in that set, but I doubt he was on the syllabus.

Anyway, by early September I know I was back in Cambridge because I remember, for some reason, that Etienne's thesis was published on Obax's birthday, which was the fifteenth of that month. The title of Etienne's thesis was: *"Thick Enough?; the Abnormal Arctic Ice of the 1890s, Including Icebergs, Ice Floes, Ice Belts, Ice Faults, Ice Folds, Ice Islands, Ice Dikes, Ice Packs, Ice Pinnacles, Ice Barriers, Ice Rafts, Ice Needles, Ice Quakes, Ice Feet, Ice Cakes, Ice Fringes, Ice Lobes, Ice Aprons, Ice Pipes, Ice Bastions, Ice Lenses, Ice*

Wedges, Ice Veins, Ice Saddles, Ice Rumples, Ice Dust, Ice Haycocks, Ice Fjords, Ice Domes, Ice Flowers, Ice Blows, Pencil Ice, Bullet Ice, Shelf Ice, Vuggy Ice, Brown Ice, Glacial-Ice Tongues, Icicles, Frazil Ice, Grease Ice, New Ice, Old Ice, Fast Ice, Rotten Ice, Bergy Bits, Ice Cubes, Frozen Water, and Sludge." According to a guy I knew at Cambridge University Press, the book was supposed to have come out that spring, but the editor rushed it, feeling strongly it was the perfect Christmas book.

"To Obax Geeddi, who has often helped me to clarify my ideas," the opening page read. "Obax was usually the first person I talked out my ideas with and as a result, my ideas were to some bit obscured."

The reason the dedication was even partly grammatical was that right after Obax had finished translating Etienne's thesis, she said good riddance to him, left the country, and in stepped Sybil Sawtell to pull the book together. You can read about all this and more in Etienne's acknowledgments, which I hugely recommend for the graphic account of Etienne and Sybil's naked romp on the St. John's Bridge of Sighs one afternoon in June. What you will not read in the acknowledgments is what became of *l'amour de Etienne et Sybil.*

Despite what you may suppose, Obax did not immediately break up with Etienne after she found out Sybil Sawtell was pregnant, but let's just say it didn't enhance *l'amour.* Obax, Oliver, and I had been volunteering at the Sponsored Leg Wax Booth at the Addenbrookes Hospital carnival fund-raiser. Obax was daubing hot wax on the calf of a hairy bloke (whose friends had pledged ten pounds each on the condition he let amateurs inflict torture on him that could possibly result in second-degree burns) when I noticed Etienne and Sybil walking past the Cholesterol Contest. They were heading toward us.

"Close your eyes," I told Obax, elbowing her in the ribs.

Obax inadvertently dripped wax down the inside of the hairy bloke's leg, close to his you-know-what. "Ow!" he said. "Ow, ow, ow, blimey ow!"

"Seven weeks!" Etienne said, planting his hand on Sybil's stomach. *"Incroyable, n'est-ce pas?"* Unfortunately, Obax opened her eyes precisely then. Etienne was grinning proudly.

When Obax fled, still holding the pot of wax, Sybil said, "Who was that woman?"

"The Lone Ranger," Oliver said to a bunch of people who didn't know what he was talking about.

The hairy bloke scootched off the waxing table to his feet. "Hey, come back!" he yelled and took off after Obax. The stiff piece of paper that had covered the table stuck to his legs. His thighs kind of stuck to each other, too. Come to think of it, I wonder if he ever got his pants back.

And still, Obax refused to ditch Etienne, though she admitted he was a creep. She always knew she shouldn't be with him, I think, but was afraid to make a move. Then one day, Obax apparently decided she'd had enough. Obax's father showed up and took her back to Somalia.

Why she took action at that point, which wasn't even the lowest point, I cannot tell you. For that matter, why does anyone wake up one morning and finally clean out the crawlspace or shoot the boss or quit the tuba or propose marriage or throw in the towel or run for alderman or make any other long-intended change? Of course, if philosophers can't figure out grains of sands, how was I, a mere graduate student, challenged even by the quest for data, supposed to answer for anything?

Eugene and Margaret returned to Cambridge in late fall and I took off as soon as I heard the news. I didn't want to be near their happiness. Besides, didn't I have some data to gather? And so, it was back to the Beans' for me.

When you are a guest in the house of your parents' friends, you are forced to behave the way your parents wished you behaved at home. There is no other way to explain the fact that I was not only in Arnie and Polly Bean's living room, watching *The Birdie and Mudge Comedy Hour* with them, but also that I stayed put as they peppered me with questions.

"That fellow your mom and dad met when they were here last year, what was his name?" said Polly Bean. "The one who was so impressive?"

Arnie Bean muted the television. "Wasn't the kid's grandfather a Nobel laureate?" he said.

Why did the Beans care so much about Eugene? I believed then and I believe now that they were doing my parents' dirty work. I may be free and easy when it comes to telling you about how I feel about Eugene, but with my parents, I had a hush-hush policy. "Nose around," I can hear my mother say to Polly Bean. "Find out if we have any basis for hope. But be subtle."

Hope was something my parents were running out of when it came to their daughter. "There are four reasons you depress us," my mother had written to me not long before I left for the Beans'. "Number one, no thesis. Number two, no job. Number three, no boyfriend. Number four, I can't remember."

"Yes, the grandfather got the Nobel in medicine," said Polly Bean. "He works in coronaries."

Certainly, I could have told the Beans everything I supposed my parents were so hot to know. "Despite the fact that Eugene said he would miss me," I could have said to Arnie and Polly Bean, "he never sent me so much as a postcard all those months he was away, whereas I sent him three letters, two postcards, and an ardent cablegram." I did not say this. Instead, I treated the Beans as if they were my own parents; in other words, I ignored them. I dragged my chair smack up to the TV, and tried to look as if I were fascinated.

But really I was brooding over the letter I had written to Eugene and Margaret just weeks earlier, welcoming them back to the country. Why had I mentioned I had a wedding present waiting for them? Not only a lie, but—

"Hate to see a grown man dry, Birdie!" Arnie Bean had turned the volume up high and the sound of Mudge was fierce. As if that were not enough, the housekeeper appeared with afternoon tea. "Are there any crisps?" said Arnie Bean, giving the once-over to the tray of scones and clotted cream.

Remember how Margaret said Eugene said Sean Shanahan said I should get actual black people to hand out my questionnaires? No, I didn't ask the housekeeper. I hired three undergraduates of color from the London School of Economics. Pat Kahari, Salome with no apparent last name, and the spokesman, Marimba Chibwe or possibly Chibwe Marimba—he said it both ways, which I came to believe was meant to knock me off balance. I hired the students to traipse around London, asking immigrants from the former British colonies questions such as "When you arrived, did you find that cricket was played more frequently or less frequently than you expected? Or did you find that it was played just as frequently as you would have thought?"

To tell you the truth, the housekeeper would have made a perfect data collector, not to mention datum itself, since my thesis was now titled "Racism and Immigration in Great Britain from the End of the Second World War to the Present, with Particular Consideration of the West Indians from Trinidad Now Living in the London Borough of Hackney and How

Their Expectations of England Compared with Their Experiences After They Arrived," and the housekeeper not only lived in Hackney, she was from Tobago, which is almost Trinidad.

(In case you're wondering: My title: 47 words. Etienne's title: 104 words.)

Oh, one more thing: I doubt the housekeeper would have decided, as did the undergraduates, to hold on to the filled-out questionnaires (all three hundred! With 178 questions each!) until I forked over an additional sum to them that was both agreed upon and paid in full before the data collecting commenced.

"I am writing to inform you," a letter that came first-class while I was at the Beans' stated, "that we are prepared to accept 25% more than what you originally gave us for the data. We also expect to be reimbursed for the transport costs, which for my part came to twenty-eight pounds!!! If we cannot come to any settlement, we are prepared to throw your data in the River Thames. I hope you will take careful consideration of this matter. Sincerely, Marimba (Chibwe)."

See what I mean about the first name/last name conundrum?

"Tell them to go to hell," said my father. I had called my parents collect to explain why I needed more money from them.

"There's no need for sarcasm," my mother said.

"How much data do you need?" my father said.

"She needs data to get her PhD," my mother said.

"What about buying half the data?" my father said.

"Are you asking her to not get a PhD?" my mother said.

"Does she know if a PhD from England has any authority in the United States?" my father said. "Let's start with that."

I started to kind of cry. "Can't you just rent out my room or something?"

"Honey," my mother said, but it wasn't clear to whom.

"How soon do you need the check?" said my father.

"She needs it right away," my mother said.

"Could you also send me some imitation butter salt?" I said.

The next day, a letter arrived, forwarded from Cambridge. I recognized the writing and had I not recognized the writing, I would have recognized the type, and had I not recognized the type, I would have recognized the stationery, and had I not recognized the stationery, I would have nevertheless known: the letter was from him. Polly Bean knew, too, I'm sure, but her divination would have come from Eugene's boldly written name above the return address. As she handed me the letter, she said, "If you ever want to entertain your school friends here, Arnie and I hope you will think of our home as your home." I did not even think of *my* home as my home.

"Okay," I said, and slipped the letter into my pocket with as much nonchalance as I had in me.

Later, out of the Beans' range, I opened the letter, careful to keep the envelope as pristine as possible. Why? I think I was always on the lookout for *objets* to display in my future Museum of Eugene.

"My singular dodo bird," Eugene had written on a notecard. "Please do not absquatulate on me. With ardent devotion from your once-again Cantabridgian." I would have preferred "devoted ardor," but that's being greedy. And it did not stop me from getting on a train that was heading to Eugene lickety-split. I told the Beans I was in urgent need of a certain book from the university library.

Remembering that I'd written Eugene about a wedding gift, I picked up whatever I could find at King's Cross station: a Big Ben snow globe, a Big Ben candelabra, and some shortbread having nothing to do with Big Ben. I doubted Eugene would like these gifts, but neither, I supposed, would Margaret, and that was half the battle. As soon as I arrived in town, I dropped off the package along with a note for Eugene.

I had given up my dorm room for the semester when I'd gone to London, so I spent the night in Libby's room. She was in Wales, visiting friends with her current flame—an Italian fellow we called the Guest because he always seemed to be squatting in someone else's digs, having none of his own. The Guest also seemed to get thrown out of places a lot and once, the story goes, had shown up at his tutor's flat with a piece of Yorkshire pudding in his suitcase. A fork was stuck in the pudding—that's how abruptly the Guest had been asked to leave.

Anyway, the very next morning, Eugene showed up. I couldn't have been dreaming because I hadn't slept. Did he come to return the gifts? So far, no. He thought it might be grand for us to take a stroll. Keep your fingers crossed.

Eugene and I sat on a wooden bench on the back lawn behind my dorm. We hadn't gotten farther than that because of the students who were occupying the office of the senior tutor as a show of support for the workers who had taken over the soybean fields in an obscure region of China and also, I have to hypothesize, to get out of tutorials. "Did I tell you that I've written a devastating critique of Elie Wiesel that will turn Holocaust studies on its head?" Eugene said. He was forced to speak up because of all the chanting. A damp gust of wind blew a cigarette wrapper into my face, but I didn't care. Eugene and I were together, just like the old days, wasn't that so? My imagination leapt as it ought not to have.

"Soybean workers *unite!*" the protesters shouted.

"Cool," I said. Loudly.

"Something, something, *fight!*" the protesters shouted. Or maybe *"bite."*

"Don't tell anyone," Eugene said. "I don't want to be scooped, especially by Bud Tygodnik. He is nothing but a circuit rider on the Holocaust jamboree."

"Of course not," I said.

Oliver Qas walked by in the leopard-looking stole usually worn by the girl who tried to resemble Vita Sackville-West. I didn't say hello because I felt that things were going too well between Eugene and me to risk interruption. My hope was that it was too noisy for Oliver to see me. I know that sounds ridiculous, but haven't you noticed, for instance, that you can't taste your food as well in a dark restaurant? Or that you have trouble hearing in the cold? It's the same thing. Except it wasn't. Oliver turned and looked right at me.

Eugene stood up. "I hate to tell you this," he said. My body tightened. Was this about the wedding gifts? Eugene squeezed my hand. "I'm supposed to take Margaret to the doctor," he said. "She's been feeling uncommonly peaked, poor thing." Eugene blew me a kiss and started to walk away. Then he stopped, seemed to remember something of great magnitude, and hurried back toward me. "My precious first edition," he said, "I nearly forgot." Eugene looked as if he might sit down beside me, but instead maintained his crouch. "Perchance, did you inadvertently leave some bagatelle at my door?"

"They're not mine," I said, but Eugene was already gone. A gust of wind shot a piece of grit into my eye, which brought me to tears.

The next train back to London, the 6:22, was not for two hours. There was nothing to do, nobody to see, and the only movie playing at the right time was *Boondock II*.

"Wish you were here or I was there," I wrote in the note I slipped under Libby's door. "Can't find my lavender eye shadow or my plaid poncho. You have them? My trenchant observation: It's impossible to be under the weather in this country because the weather always one downs you."

At the station, I killed time by writing a postcard to my parents. "Thought you should know," I wrote, "that early in the life of Anwar Sadat, the former president of Egypt and winner of the Nobel Prize for Peace entered a talent show boasting that he could do Western and belly dancing as well as make animal noises! I read this in a newspaper editorial. Love from your penniless and pence-i-less (ha-ha) daughter." This was my way of showing sincere gratitude.

It was 5:46. "May I have the next train?" I heard Oliver say in back of me.

I could have played along. I could have said, "The next train is a waltz" or "My train card is full" or anything. Oliver had been a real pal, more than any other young man in my life had ever been. Did I tell you that in our days of riding the train, he would always tidy up the lavatory before I used it? Or that when I lost his brother's bicycle, Oliver bought an identical bike to give his brother and told me that the old one had turned up? (I met his brother last year and figured it out, but that's another story.) Of all the friends of mine who hated Eugene, Oliver's hatred meant the most to me.

I knew that Oliver was probably right about Eugene, whom he called "your heinous hypnotist" because he couldn't bring himself to utter Eugene's name. I also knew that sooner or later Oliver's patience with my Eugene-centricity was likely to come to an end and I would have to choose between Oliver and Eugene. Oliver didn't understand how I felt about Eugene, or maybe he did. I'm not excusing myself for what I did; I'm just explaining.

What I did when I heard Oliver ask me for the next train,

and when I looked at him looking at me, was to say: "Why are you wearing that ludicrous stole?"

Oliver blinked many times. I should have said that I was sorry because I truly was; and I should have thanked him for being so benevolent because he unfailingly was; and I should have said that I realized he was wearing a Persian lamb mantle, not a ludicrous stole; but somehow, it slipped my mind that saying anything was a possibility. I wasn't even able to move, let alone speak.

I couldn't tell you how long we stood there, saying nothing, but eventually my train pulled up and I stepped inside. "I believe this is the end of the line, then," Oliver said. He kissed me on the cheek. I looked for him as the train chugged out of the station, but I never saw him on the platform. I never saw Oliver Qas again.

He didn't return to school and I never could track him down. So I guess I did choose between Eugene and Oliver, and maybe you think I chose wrong.

Had I only been more kind. That's what haunted me while riding the 6:22 and that's what would haunt me a week later as I sat in the LSE cafeteria, drinking cup after cup of coffee, waiting with my parents' check in my tote bag for the brats to arrive and hand over my data. That's also what turned out to haunt me just a few years ago when I heard that Oliver Qas had died in a terrible meat fondue accident.

So there I sat on a broken chair, in a smoky room, feeling rueful and ashamed and nostalgic, and also jittery from the caffeine. Naturally, Marimba Chibwe (or Chibwe Marimba) and his posse were late. I jumped up with a start. Where was my tote bag? My tote bag contained not only my parents' check, but the single copy of what I'd written so far of my thesis, a postcard from Eugene telling me he would be "moved" if I would attend his "Problems in Truth" seminar, a picture of Eugene and me at his talk "What Puppetry Can Teach Philosophers," my wallet, my passport, keys to the Beans', and who knows what else. The tote bag had vanished.

I was absolutely hysterical by the time the data collectors showed up. This was not the most strategic way to greet your adversaries. I tried to compose myself. "Nice bag," said Marimba or Chibwe, indicating the tote bag that had apparently been on my arm the whole time. Wow. Could things be turning around for me?

Maybe not yet. When the data collectors surrendered the data, they made me sign a piece of paper that guaranteed them royalties should my thesis ever become a book. Cheeky, wot?

Back at Cambridge, I sublet a flat that belonged to a former fling of Libby's, then on tour in Wales as the reigning tiddledywinks champion of England. He was the one who told Libby, "For me, every night is New Year's Eve!" The flat was mine for three months, ample time, I thought, to analyze my data, or at least sort it into piles. I was grateful for the monotonous diversion.

The day I moved in, I ran into Eugene and Margaret on the stairs. Did I mention that the flat I'd found was conveniently located directly above theirs? Choosing to live in spitting distance of both your beloved and his beloved is asking for it, but you know me—always asking for it. Eugene and Margaret were lugging groceries for a curry party they would throw that night. From the smell of it, they seemed to have curry parties every night and from the sound of it, they were merry occasions, featuring lively games of charades in which the players acted out the titles of Greek tragedies. I was not invited to any of the parties.

"It's kismet!" I said with fake delight when Eugene, Margaret, and I discovered I was to be living within curry-smelling distance of them. I swear to God, I don't even know what the word "kismet" means. I figured it was a friendly thing to say. Margaret wheezed a little and Eugene patted her on the back. Hypochondriacs make me sick.

"Would it be okay if my sister wrote to you with a few questions relating to her thesis?" said a recovered Margaret.

"Me?" I said.

"She's a graduate student in anthropology at Berkeley," Margaret said.

"That's nice," I said.

"She's writing her thesis about Eugene's and my wedding and she'd like to include some quotes from the broader social network."

"Oh," I said. "I mean, sure."

"Am finally on top of Eugene!" I wrote to Libby. "But not the way you think. Will explain later. Meantime, have you seen my plaid poncho?" As I was slipping the note under Libby's door, she showed up in tears, holding a slightly bloody pillow. "He kicked me out," she said.

"He kicked you out of Wales!" I said.

"No, no, not the Guest. We came back from Wales this morning," Libby said. "Dr. Fleissig." (Don't worry, you'll catch up in a second.)

"Before your fifty minutes were up?" I said.

"He went queasy because I got blood on his analytic pillow," Libby said. "He actually demanded I quote unquote 'depollute' it."

"But he's a shrink," I said.

"Seems he has a phobia about bodily functions," Libby said.

Libby had been seeing Dr. Fleissig for about a year. "That's a rather short skirt, my dear," Libby had told me Dr. Fleissig said as soon as she sat down during the first session. "Nonverbal communication, I presume," he had said. Libby had decided to go to a psychiatrist in the first place because she wanted to explore why she was so vulnerable to the advances of men. The next thing Libby knew, she and Dr. Fleissig had a standing appointment on the couch, though "standing" is perhaps a poor word choice.

"Is this ethical?" Libby had asked Dr. Fleissig.

"Yes," said Dr. Fleissig, "because I'm charging you."

"Bloody Dr. Fleissig," said Libby, putting down the pillow.

"They say you can get out a bloodstain by blotting it with peroxide, detergent, and vinegar, in equal parts," I said.

Libby picked up the pillow and scrutinized the spot. Then, she walked dramatically to the window, opened it wide, and threw the pillow to the wind. "Toodle-oo, transference," she said. In the days I lived across the courtyard from Libby, an open window meant the guy was finally gone, come on over.

"On second thought," I said, "that's how you remove gravy.

"Are you going to miss him?" I said.

"Only for one thing," Libby said. "And I think you know what that is."

"His ennnnnnnndless . . ." I said.

"Supply of Valium," Libby said.

May I ask you a question? Does it seem to you that something was awry in that exchange between Libby and me? Maybe you are more perspicacious than I am, but I believed that Libby and I were the best of pals, that everything about us was, and always would remain, easy-peasy. We may have had problems with the world, but never with each other. That's what I thought.

Imagine how bowled over I was the next day, then, when I

received the following note from Libby: "I will scour my room early this week (by Weds) and return your eye shadow, your plaid poncho, your broken kettle, and anything else that could possibly be construed as yours. I will admit to not taking inventories of my own things and hence I do not keep constant track of what belongs to you in my room, which incidentally you have been using to type your thesis in. To be accused like this is really too much. Your sincerely confused, bothered, and bewildered, Libby."

To be accused of being an accuser was also too much. This was the most anyone had ever seemed to hate me and I didn't like it one little bit, no matter how hard I tried to believe the note was a side-effect of Valium withdrawal.

The day Libby's note came was the same day Eugene and Margaret brought home a puppy called Mr. Softie. From the vestibule in my flat, I could hear Eugene and Margaret on the steps cooing over the dog. If you are in a paranoid mood to begin with, you can easily imagine that two adults talking tenderly to a dog are in fact talking to each other.

Things had not been going my way for a while but now they were really not going my way. Mr. Softie's arrival proved to me that things would get even worse. Before I moved to England, everything had always gone my way and it never occurred to me that would come to an end. Make that: before I met Eugene.

How much worse could it get? I pictured myself, a long time from now, decrepit and still sorting my data in the university library. "See that old lady," an undergrad would say to her companion, "there is a legend that she's been here a hundred years! She doesn't have a single friend. She alienated them all."

That reminds me: Do you remember my telling you a while ago about the ancient-looking man that Eugene and I had seen one day in the university library? This was in the day when things seemed hunky-dory. I certainly regret now that I laughed at that old man.

What was the point of staying in this place? There was hardly anyone left to tell. There was only one person.

"You're saying, if I hear you correctly, that you'd like to abandon ship, pack it in, call it a day, throw in the towel, vacate the premises—put simply, proclaim to the world that you are a quitter?" Sean Shanahan said. He poured two glasses of sherry. "Sherry?" he said.

"No," I said, "I mean no to the sherry, not to the towel and the other stuff you said." I fiddled with the zipper on my jacket. Besides the green down jacket, I was wearing corduroy jeans, cowboy boots, and a ridiculous headband. As I used to say, I was in my Ugly American phase. Also, though I didn't say it, my ugly phase.

"Hmmmmm," Sean Shanahan said, downing sherry number one. "Have you discussed this with Eugene?"

"You know what?" I said. I pulled up the zipper on my jacket. "I have to go."

As I was walking out the door, Sean Shanahan sighed. "Are you aware that this means I personally must fill out numerous forms?" he said. Sean Shanahan took a slug of sherry number two and I vacated the premises once and for all.

"Tell them Anne Frank is ringing up," I said to the overseas operator. When I first arrived in Cambridge, I had come up with an elaborate code for sending messages to my parents based on what name I used when I reversed the charges. Shirley Temple meant "everything dandy." Amelia Earhart meant "arrived safely." Mrs. A. Einstein meant "I have a question but it's relatively unimportant." Joan of Arc meant . . . gee, it couldn't have been "It's hot here"—could it? I don't remember. But Anne Frank was a definite call for help. My parents never did master the code. They said yes to every operator.

"To be honest, I never bought the whole idea of academia," my father said when I broke the news that I was coming home. This was a generous stab at revisionist history, since my father had, in fact, literally bought the whole idea of academia. He drank from a Cambridge mug, wrote with a Cambridge pen, hung a Cambridge pennant in his office, and, to my mortification, had a Cambridge bumper sticker plastered on his car. He also gave my grandmother a Cambridge sweatshirt, which she wore, being as enthusiastic as her son was about my illustrious higher education. "Look at the Gillespie girl," my father said now. "She's been trapped at Swarthmore for, what, ten years and she has nothing to show for it except a job."

"It's Middlebury," said my mother to my father. Then to me, she said, "We're thrilled you're coming back. Why don't you think about getting an op-ed published in the *Times* about your experience—'A Yank in Cambridge'?"

I grunted in a way that gave away nothing. "I made reservations for Tuesday," I said.

"My only regret," said my father, "is that you didn't marry a European prince. That would have been the one wedding I wouldn't have had to pay for."

"Leave her alone," my mother said to my father.

"Is there a ban against humor?" my father said.

"That was not humor," said my mother. "That was teasing."

"We'll be at the airport Tuesday," my father said.

"Before you leave the country," my mother said, "do you think you should buy a cashmere sweater for yourself at the Argyle Hut? I heard they're on sale and I'll give you my charge card."

"Okay," I said.

"It's not too late to go to medical school, you know," my father said.

"Bye. Thanks," I said. There had been no mention of the data they had paid for, and for that, I was grateful.

About seven seconds after I hung up, the phone rang.

"I forgot to tell you," my mother said, "we were at a dinner party last night at the McGraths' and I met a woman whose daughter is at Cambridge. She has something to do with Hellenistic studies and she's very smart."

"Do you know her?" my father said.

"Her name is Margaret," my mother said. "I promised you'd look her up."

The next day, I stuffed my data into many mailing bags and shipped them to Philadelphia. On the way back from the post office, I wrote a schmaltzy note for Libby, in which I lied and told her I'd found my plaid poncho. I put the note in her college pigeonhole, then took it out and tore it up.

That night, to quote Sean Shanahan, I vacated the premises, spending the night with the Beans before taking an early flight home. As I waited outside for a taxi to the Cambridge train station, an ambulance screeched up to the building. Two emergency workers rushed inside and, soon after, brought Margaret down on a stretcher. Eugene walked alongside, but he didn't seem to pay attention to Margaret.

"What happened?" I said to Eugene.

"You mean this time?" Eugene said. He sighed. "Apollinaire said sickness is the vacation of the poor."

How much would you hate me if I told you I was happy?

Weeks later, when the mailing bags arrived in Philadelphia, they were dog-eared and ripped open, much of the gray insulation had come out, and a lot of my data was smudged and ruined. They looked like miniature body bags shipped from a war zone.

I picked up one of the relatively intact questionnaires and read a question, I swear at random. "If the government implemented a forced repatriation scheme in the near future, offering monetary compensation, what do you think you would do?" The respondent had written (or had dictated to one of the data collectors): "If the monetary was large enough, I would take it and run." I did not feel the need to read any more data.

I do have one bit of propitious news. According to my sources, Etienne and Sybil Sawtell became engaged a month before their baby was due, but Monsieur et Madame Sawtell broke it off on the grounds that Etienne was too bourgeois, thus either proving or disproving Etienne's argument that class matters.

You know who would have gotten a big kick out of that? Oliver Qas.

Part 2

HER

SIX

"Did you read her audition sketches?" my mother said.

"I read them," my father said. "They're not very good."

"They're terrible," my mother said. "She's not going to get the job."

"What will become of her?" my father said. "She has no PhD, no skills, no prospects."

My parents were in the bedroom and I was in the living room, which doubled as my bedroom in the tiny apartment they'd been renting while the town house they'd bought a few months earlier was being restored to the eighteenth century, and the burglar alarm, central air-conditioning, and whole-house vacuum cleaner system were installed. When my parents signed the lease to the apartment, they hadn't counted on their grown-up daughter, then three thousand miles away, living there as well. Nor had they apparently known then or probably ever how easy it was to hear a conversation through the walls.

As my parents kept on talking about me in the next room, I

lay on the bed, staring at the labels on the cartons of books opposite me: "Fiction (*A–B, also U*)"; "Fiction (underlined)"; "Fiction (throw away?)"; "Antiques (not 20th Century!)"; "Britannica
Encyclopaedias (torn, *R–Z,* not *S*)"; "The Holocaust & Mis-
cellaneous"; "The West (American)"; "Foreign"; "Essays (Mon-
taigne)"; "Dictionaries, Cookbooks, Saul Bellow"; "Biographies
of Dead People"; "Poetry, Rhyming"; "Churchill & U Thant &
Diet—Oversize"; "Catalogs—Possibly Valuable"; "S & H Green
Stamps Books (collectible?)"; "Paperbacks Not Worth Saving";
"Travel—Sunny Places Only"; "Boxed Books—This Side Up";
"Psychology Textbooks (obsolete?)"; "Library Books (Thor
Heyerdahl, *Velvet-Colored Brick,* etc.)"; "College Spanish";
"Unreadable"; "Satire????"; "Books to Prop Up Yellow Table."

"Why did you tell her to go to Cambridge in the first
place?" my mother said. She was not the only one interested in
the answer. So as not to miss a word, I tiptoed to the wall that
separated us and stood frozen, nervous that my parents would
hear me and stop talking.

"I never told her that," my father said. "I always thought she
should go to medical school." I muffled a sneeze. The cartons
were dusty.

"Didn't you tell her Cambridge had more Nobel winners
than any other school in the world?" my mother said.

"If I did, I didn't mean anything by it," my father said,
"though it happens to be true."

"And that the English had beautiful complexions," my
mother said.

"Don't they?" my father said.

Ho-hum. This was old news. I tiptoed back to the bed and
sat down. In point of fact, my father certainly did dream of my
becoming a doctor, marrying a doctor, and having a doctor's
children.

"What does she do all day?" my father said. "She's been back from England for months. Is she really working on her thesis?"

"I think she waits around to see if she got the job," my mother said.

"That can't be healthy," my father said.

"There's no need to be so hard on her," my mother said. "I read an article that said this generation is the most immature generation in history."

"Do you really buy that?" my father said. "Look at all the kids out there in law school and medical school. I find it hard to believe that an entire generation failed to turn in their theses. It can't be normal."

"You're the one who let her quit the psychiatrist," my mother said.

"Let her?" my father said. "She's twenty-three years old. Who could stop her?"

My father had lately been in the habit of reminding my mother and me—and I suppose himself—of my age. "You're twenty-three years old and you won't wear a coat when your mother tells you it's cold outside?" "You're twenty-three years old and you'd rather stay home and watch TV than go to the Wolitzers' house for dinner with us?" "You're twenty-three years old and you don't like halibut?" We all knew, of course, what he really meant: "You're twenty-three years old and you're living at home!" It was an excellent point.

"You cannot deny that you were very discouraging about the psychiatrist," my mother said.

"Frankly, the situation seemed hopeless," my father said. Then I heard him correcting himself. "*Seems* hopeless."

The conversation was turning into one I didn't want to overhear. But how could I extricate myself? If my parents knew

I was leaving, I was sure they would put two and two together and figure out I had picked up every word of their tête-à-tête. Unfortunately, the apartment was configured in such a way that I could not exit unseen unless I jumped out of the window. This wasn't the worst idea. We were on the tenth floor.

"You didn't give her therapy a chance," my mother said. "Walt says therapy takes six months to work." Uncle Walt was my mother's cousin. My parents considered him the last word in medicine by virtue of his being a podiatrist.

"But she's smart," my father said. "She should have been able to do it in six weeks."

Yes, I suppose I could have taken this as a tribute. But I didn't. What if I made a noise, I wondered—turned on the TV, screeched a chair across the floor, pushed over a lamp, coughed? Would my parents remember I was nearby and shut up? I gave up and put a pillow over my head. (Have you noticed how that never works?)

The job my parents were so gloomy about my getting was that of staff writer for a sketch-comedy TV show in New York. No, not *Saturday Night Live*—the other show, *Taped But Proud*. If my aunt Sugar (Uncle Walt's wife) hadn't known the associate producer, there is no way I could have finagled an interview with the executive producer, Archie Durkin. The interview lasted only a few minutes and most of the time, Archie Durkin stared at the form I'd filled out in the waiting room. After all that taking in of my address, phone number, social security number, and previous experience (none), Archie Durkin, his eyes still on the page, said, "Is this your real name or a stage name?" Archie Durkin pronounced his *a*'s the same way Eugene did, so I automatically liked him.

"Huh?" I said. Archie Durkin never answered because just then his pretty assistant came in without knocking and told him that week's host had walked out because the grapes in her dressing room had been washed in tap water, not mineral water as had been specified in her contract. As he listened, Archie Durkin stroked the top of his head the way men who have a comb-over seem to do, except he had a full head of hair. When the assistant left, Archie Durkin picked up the phone and as he was dialing said to me, "Think you could have three sketches for me by Friday?"

It was Monday. Mister, I thought, I couldn't give you one sketch, even if I had until forever. "Sure," I said. "No problem."

Archie Durkin's assistant led me to the elevator. "That's where we shot the famous midget and cattle sketch," she said, indicating a closed door.

"I must have been living in England when that was on, I mean, aired," I said. Near the door was a sofa on which someone was out cold in a dinosaur-themed sleeping bag.

"That's where we microwave takeout, mostly pizza, and smoke grass and stuff," the assistant said as we passed a filthy little kitchen.

"In England, they call takeout 'takeaway,' " I said to support my claim that I'd been in England during the midget sketch. My remark went unacknowledged.

"You want to see a writer's office?" the assistant said, opening a door to a nice-sized room where a guy, presumably a writer, was standing by an open window, smoking a cigarette and talking on the phone.

This place was so cool! I really wanted to write for *Taped But Proud*.

"According to Aunt Sugar's producer friend, it's impossible to get a job there," my mother said. She and my father had picked me up at the train station after the interview and we were in the car on our way to dinner. "Even though the show's bad, everyone wants to work there, or so I'm told by Aunt Sugar. There's a space; isn't that a space?"

My father jerked the car to a stop. "That's a hydrant," he said, disgusted. "The city is riddled with them." My father sped ahead, faster than it befits one who is looking for a parking spot.

"But I'm sure you'll get the job," my mother said. For a trillion reasons, this was not encouraging.

"She better get it," my father said. "Is that guy leaving?"

"She's very talented," my mother said. "No, he's putting things in the car." She turned to me in the backseat. "But you shouldn't have worn blue jeans to the interview."

"Mom, Archie was wearing blue jeans," I said.

"What Archie Durkin was wearing is not relevant," my mother said. "He already has the job."

"You're sure he's not putting things in the car because he's leaving?" my father said, slowing the car down. In back of us, plenty of honking was going on.

"He's not leaving," my mother said.

"Archie Durkin's assistant said they probably needed girl writers because they don't have any," I said. "So that's something."

"What kind of a cockamamie name is Archie Durkin?" my father said. "Do you think I can get into that space?"

"It could be a stage name," I said.

"Didn't I tell you not to wear blue jeans?" my mother said. "Anyone who's going anywhere does not wear blue jeans."

"What's the difference what she wore? Lots of people wear dungarees these days. Norman wears them to work," my father said. "I'm going to try to get into that space." My father backed the car up with a punch.

"All I know is that everyone was wearing blue jeans at the show," I said.

"Forget it," my father said. "I'll never get in there. Why don't we go to Lu Yuk? There's always parking around there." My father raced to make the light, which was turning from yellow to red.

"I can drop you off and park somewhere and walk to the Oyster Box," I said. "I don't mind at all."

"She can't walk," my mother said. We ended up at a place called Lorna Paul's, where we just about parked on top of the table.

That night, after my parents were asleep, that's when I started to write my sketches. They had to do with an adult living at home with her parents. And my mother and father were correct: the sketches, I have come to realize, were terrible. So much for "Write what you know."

By my calculations, the FedEx package with my sketches arrived at the *Taped But Proud* offices between 10 A.M. and 2 P.M. on Thursday. I gave Archie Durkin precisely a week to read the sketches, and thereafter, called his office three days a week at 2 P.M., varying the days so it wouldn't appear too clockworky. This wasn't my idea. It was pressed on me by a guy called Corby O'Donnell-McDonald, who lived in Maine as a lobsterman/actor. He was the friend of one of my high school friends and I had called him for advice on her recommendation. According to my friend, Corby was a wizard when it came to figuring out the best way to make a potential employer hire you. Corby was currently unemployed, so I'm not sure why I had so much faith; but he talked with greater certainty than circumstances warranted, and I am a sucker for that.

"Okay, here's what happened," I would say to Corby immediately after I called *Taped But Proud*. I had never actually met Corby, but was in constant phone consultation with him about my chances of getting the job.

"The phone rang three times," I would say to Corby. "Then an assistant picked up and said, 'Please hold.' "

"Which assistant?" Corby would say. "The one with the lisp?"

"No. The one who doesn't always recognize my voice," I would say.

"Okay, so . . ." Corby would say.

"Then I'd guess I waited about a minute," I would say.

"About a minute?" Corby would say.

"I don't know for sure," I would say, "because I pushed the wrong button on the stopwatch. Then the assistant came back and said hello again and I asked to speak to Archie Durkin. Then she asked who was calling so I said my name."

"Excellent," Corby would say.

"Then," I would say, "she said, 'Oh, hello.' "

"What was her tone?" Corby would say.

"Like she knew something but wasn't allowed to tell me," I would say. "Then I waited for ninety-four seconds—"

"Did she put you on hold or put the phone down?" Corby would say.

"Good point," I would say. "She must have put the phone down because I could hear Archie Durkin talking in the background but I couldn't make out what he was saying."

"And you're sure it was Archie Durkin?" Corby would say.

"Not absolutely sure," I would say.

"That's important," Corby would say. "Then what happened?"

"The assistant came back and she said he was in a meeting, but she kind of overenunciated the word 'mee-ting,' " I would say. "You know what I mean?"

"Yes, I do," Corby would say.

"She sounded a tiny bit flustered," I would say.

"I have to be honest," Corby would say. "That worries me."

"So what do you think? Do you think I didn't get the job?" I would say.

Corby would pause and then he would say, with a very measured voice, "The good news is that you definitely didn't blow it."

"Really?" I would say.

"But I need more information," Corby would say. "Here's what. Next time, call in the morning to throw them off balance."

And so I did, though to no avail. Archie Durkin, as was reported by the assistant who had a lisp, "wath not at hith dethk." Both Corby and I were suspicious. One hundred and thirty-three seconds, we agreed, had been longer than one needed to determine that Archie Durkin was not at his desk, even for someone with a lisp.

The next morning, while my mother, father, and I were, as usual, looking for the keys to the car so that my parents could leave for work and I could remain in the apartment and do nothing under the pretense of working on my thesis, my father said to me, "I'm going to bring it up just one more time: Why don't you call the damn show and ask if you got the job?"

I lifted the cushions on the sofa, pretending to be engrossed in the search for the keys. "She doesn't want to jinx her chances," my mother said.

"That's ridiculous," my father said. Then, to my mother: "You're sure they're not in some pocket of your pocketbook?"

"People don't like pain-in-the-necks," I said.

"People don't refuse to hire someone because she wonders if she has a job," my father said.

"Okay, if you tell me what both of you were wearing last night, I'll go check the pockets," I said.

"Just a minute," my father said to me. "Didn't I give the keys back to you after we came back from the Kerreys'?" he said to my mother. "Think."

"You know, it *is* odd that you haven't heard anything," my mother said. "It's been a long time."

"Is it possible they forgot about you?" my father said. "Did the producer take notes during the interview—you know, make some sort of record?"

"They don't do that in TV," I said, without any idea what I was talking about. "They never write things down."

"Would you like me to call Archie Durkin?" my father said. "Because I don't have a problem with that." I rolled my eyes. He wasn't kidding.

"On another subject," my mother said, "Daddy and I were thinking maybe you should go back to that psychiatrist."

"Uncle Walt says he seriously doubts that Debby would have ever gotten married if she hadn't been in therapy," my father said.

Both my mother and father looked at me with what seemed to be great interest. I gave them my trusty old indecisive grunt. "I bet the keys are in the car," I said. "Want me to check?"

Though they may have not realized this, my parents were getting off easy. What I could have let slip was that Dr. Kropotkin, the shrink Uncle Walt had recommended so highly, had said to me during our first session, "Well, Freud would have had a shit fit if he heard what I'm about to tell you, but here goes nothing. My advice is: Do whatever it takes to get out of that place; borrow money if you have to." The place she was referring to was the tiny temporary apartment I was living in with my parents. "It's an unhealthy situation," Dr. Kropotkin had said. Then she added—and my father might have appreciated this—"for someone who, may I remind you, my dear, is twenty-three."

During the second session, Dr. Kropotkin offered to lend me

money herself. What's more, she had set out a plate of homemade brownies and told me to help myself. All in all, I don't think Freud would have been so happy with the second session, either.

The other news I could have shared with my parents was that yes, Debby did get married, but her husband, I knew for a fact, was a homosexual.

But I didn't say any of this. I'm obnoxious, but not that obnoxious. I'm also, as you may have noticed, a bit passive. Not entirely passive, however. For after Corby and I had gone over the nuances of Archie's alleged absence at his desk, I felt in need of a pick-me-up. And so this time, I did not hang up after dialing all fifteen digits of Eugene's phone number.

"Did I wake you?" I said to Margaret. There is always displeasure when one discerns that it is the spouse and not the person one wanted to talk to who has answered the phone. This was worse, though, because I had hoped that by this time Margaret was, pardon me, dead. Or at least on her way out. When I'd seen her last, she was lying on a stretcher, remember? There better not be a God because I'll be in big trouble.

On top of everything else, it was costing me who-knows-what a minute. Actually, the bill would fall to my parents, but that's academic.

"I was just dozing," Margaret said. She yawned in what I considered a flagrant way, but I refused to feel guilty. It was 8 P.M. her time. Margaret and I chitchatted until I interrupted to fake an afterthought. "Hey," I said, "is Eugene around?" The effect I was going for was as-if-I-care.

"He didn't call you?" Margaret said. "I thought he said he was going to call you. He's at a conference in Washington. On furry logic."

That Eugene was geographically closer to me in Philadelphia than Margaret in Cambridge, England, afforded me a strange comfort. "And how are you?" I said, figuring I might as well get some extra credit with Margaret.

"To be honest," Margaret said, "the bed rest has gotten me a tad down."

"Bed rest?" I said with hope.

"Eugene didn't tell you we were pregnant?" Margaret said. "I swore he said he was going to call you."

The strange comfort, the extra credit, the hope: all of it now gone. "Congratulations," I said.

"Thank you," Margaret said. "You're sweet. We found out the day I was rushed to the hospital. Wasn't that the day you left England?"

That night, after dinner, I muttered to my parents, "So I guess I could see Dr. Kropotkin." I noticed my mother steal a look at my father and grin ever so slightly. To communicate what to him? Relief? Victory? "Only a few times, though," I said firmly.

"Walt says analysis can make you crazy before it cures you, but that's a lot of hooey," my father said.

"We could do a family session," my mother said. "Is that something we should think about? That is, if it would help. But I couldn't do it until after five. I've got to keep my eye on the contractor."

"I see no need to sit around and rehash our past together," my father said. "What's done is done." Even my father must have known that this position did not exactly capture the spirit of analytic inquiry.

"Yes, but you know how everyone's always talking about dysfunctional families," my mother said.

"That's baloney," my father said. "Dysfunctional families work just fine."

A friend of mine had once told me that what you realize after a hundred thousand dollars' worth of therapy is that the parent you thought you had a problem with is not in fact where the problem lies; it is with the other one. I could not work out what this meant in my case.

"I'm thinking Dr. Kropotkin might be a good sounding board," I said, "as far as my thesis goes, I mean." It just then occurred to me that not once during any of my sessions with Dr. Kropotkin had Eugene's name ever come up.

"Did Sean Shanahan read the pages you sent him?" my mother said. I guess I don't have to tell you that I hadn't sent Sean Shanahan a single page.

"Oh, that reminds me," I said. "I called Sean Shanahan today."

"Does he think you have enough data?" my father said.

"I talked for more than a few minutes," I said. "I hope that's okay."

"Of course, sweetheart," my mother said. "What did he think about what you sent him? Did he like it?" She gave me the look you would give the airline representative who is reading the list of deaths and survivors from the plane crash your beloved was on.

"He thought that the logic of the last stuff I sent him was a little furry," I said.

"Oh?" my father said, now having yet one more thing to be agitated about.

"Oh, no," my mother said.

"But it's okay," I said.

"You fixed it?" my mother said.

"Definitely," I said. "Yes, sir."

"Who wants to go for ice cream?" my father said, with the air of someone who wants to leave the scene before there is any more news.

"Do you think we should?" my mother said. "We have such a good parking space."

"What the hell," my father said.

We did go for ice cream, and when we returned to the apartment, we found a spot right out front. Furthermore, there was a message on my parents' brand-new phone machine, the machine with millions of buttons on which my father formally declared that he and my mother were not home and that he hoped he was using "this thing" correctly while in the background, my mother enunciated in a stage whisper to my father, "Just talk into the microphone, dear."

"Hi, there," the incoming message boomed, "it's Archie Durkin and if your daughter can get up to New York this coming Monday, *Taped But Proud* would be thrilled to have her as a staff writer. If she has an agent, tell him to call Business Affairs. I'm assuming you're the *proud* parents but if you're not, watch the show anyway. Friday at midnight on CBS. We were nominated for an Emmy."

I had the job! How exciting to be in a world where someone assumed that there was even a possibility I had an agent!

"Hip hip hooray!" my father said.

"I knew you would get it!" my mother said, then after a moment: "Can anything go wrong? You don't think it was a prank, do you?"

"If only there were a way to save the message," my father said, examining the machine from a safe distance. Of course there was a way, but none of us was technically advanced enough to know it. "Wait until I tell Walt," he said.

The next day, after my parents left for work after we looked for the keys to the car, I immediately called Corby and told him the good news. "Give me the message verbatim," Corby said.

And I did, after which I said, "Can anything go wrong?"

Corby paused for a long time and then he said, "I'd bet money on it."

"I knew it," I said. "Nothing ever turns out right."

"I meant in the long run," said Corby. "Wrong in the long run."

I beamed. "I was wondering," I said, "do you think it would be a good idea for us to meet one of these days?"

"You mean in the flesh?" Corby said.

"I was picturing face-to-face to start with," I said.

"Mm," Corby said. "I kind of like it this way. It's very professional."

"Yeah," I said. "You might be right. Being in close quarters with people can be so sticky."

SEVEN

"You have to help me," I said in a snivel to my mother over the phone. It was one thirty in the morning and I was in my office at *Taped But Proud,* having been on the job for not even four whole days. "I'm supposed to write a sketch by tomorrow about Belarus." I wiped away tears with my sleeve. "And it has to be funny."

"A sketch about Belarus?" my mother said.

"They tortured a journalist because he was criticizing the government," I said. "A sketch about that. It has to be topical."

"Well, let's see," my mother said. "Belarus has a very poor human rights record."

"I know *that,*" I said with a sigh. "But can you think of something funny about the situation?" My mother didn't say anything.

"There was also a siege on an orphanage in Belarus. A few children were killed, I think. It could be about that," I said as if I were being helpful, "but it still has to be really, really funny."

"Hold on," my mother said, putting the phone down.

"Wake up," I heard her say in the background. "We have to write a sketch about Belarus."

"Belarus?" I heard my father say to my mother in a groggy voice. "What about Belarus?"

"Something funny about the situation there," my mother said. "It has to be topical."

"What time is it?" I heard my father say.

"Here," I heard my mother say. "You talk to her."

"Let me get this straight," my father said to me. "You have to write something about Belarus?"

"I need at least three pages," I said.

"Wait a minute," my father said. "I can't think unless I'm dressed."

My mother picked up the phone. "Isn't there someone at the show who could help you?" she said.

"No. I mean yes," I said, "but I can't ask anyone anything. They think I know how to write. I tricked them."

"You're a very good writer," my mother said.

"First my thesis, now this," I said.

"Okay," my mother said. "What if . . . don't worry . . . Wait, I just thought of something." My mother must have pressed the button on the intercom because I heard a low-pitched tone. In my parents' new house, there was an intercom in every room. "Mother," I heard my mother say. My grandmother was staying with my parents for a few weeks. "Are you up?" my mother said. "Mother, wake up. We're going to meet in the den to write a sketch about the Old Country for *Taped But Proud.*"

"But Grandma doesn't know how to write a sketch," I said.

"Yes, but her grandmother's from Romania and she's awake," my mother said. "We'll call you back in a little while."

"When?" I said. I said that before my mother had finished her sentence.

"We just have to think," my mother said. "We'll come up with something." I could hear my father in the background. "Daddy wants to know if Poland could be in the sketch."

"Sure. Fine," I said, "as long as it's really, really funny. And three pages."

I stared at my computer. Some time went by. It always does. The phone rang. It was my father. "What if you had the Poles storming the whatever, intending to free the journalist, but they fail because they're such nincompoops? You could enact every Polish joke in the book, starting with changing a lightbulb."

"Hmm," I said and then I didn't say anything else.

"Grandma thinks it's funny," my father said eventually.

"They don't seem to like ideas that are quote 'too jokey' here," I said.

"Isn't jokey the point?" my father said.

The writer I shared an office with, Frick Rips, returned from walking his dog. Frick was allowed to have a dog in the building because he'd paid a doctor to write a letter saying that Frick was blind. "Gotta go, writers' meeting, can't talk," I said to my father with dispatch and slammed the phone down.

The next morning, after a read-through of the Belarus sketches, at which I truly believe my sketch was the worst, Joyce Slutzky called me into her office. Joyce Slutzky, beloved companion of Archie Durkin, dedicated protector of Grover the parrot, and former dental hygienist, was also, in effect, the producer of *Taped But Proud*. Certainly, Joyce Slutzky had the power to fire me.

"Have a seat," she said, "and a juice." Joyce Slutzky had an assistant who appeared to have no other role than to make sure her boss was supplied with fresh-squeezed vegetable juice around the clock. The juicer was in the bathroom.

To be polite, I took a juice. "Now, about your Belarus

sketch," Joyce Slutzky said. In an attempt to look as if I didn't think I was going to lose my job then and there, I waved my hand to say, "Pshaw." The gesture, I'm thinking now, might have come off as a little supercilious. "To have General what's-his-name do all those Polish jokes is so obvious," Joyce Slutzky said. She stopped to drink up her juice. I, meanwhile, deliberated about whether it made me look better or worse to tell her that the sketch was completely my father's idea. Before I made up my mind about blaming my father, Joyce Slutzky said, "It's such a 'why didn't I think of that?' thing. You're a genius!"

I smiled wide. Joyce Slutzky, of course, did not realize how much of a "why didn't I think of that?" thing that thing really was. "Unfortunately," she said, "we can't use it because *Saturday Night Live* is supposedly doing a Belarus cold open next week."

"That's show biz," I said, full of buoyancy. As long as I still had a job, I didn't care what they did with my Belarus sketch.

"Can I ask you a personal question?" Joyce Slutzky said. "Are you seeing anyone?"

"Unh, no," I said. She wasn't going to send me into therapy, was she? For Dr. Kropotkin was as much as I could handle on that score.

"It's just that I know Dwayne Schmokler's lawyer," Joyce Slutzky said. "You know who Dwayne Schmokler is?"

"The editor of *Wet* magazine?" I said.

"Bingo," Joyce Slutzky said. "I was thinking of fixing you up with his attorney-at-law. I know he'd really like you."

"Thanks," I said. What else could I say?

"It's so nice finally to have a girl writer on the staff," Joyce Slutzky said. "I told Yolanda about you, and she said you're going to do very well here." Yolanda was Joyce Slutzky's psychic and she ruled. That is, she ruled Joyce Slutzky and Joyce Slutzky ruled everyone working at *Taped But Proud,* most of all Archie

Durkin. In fact, at that very moment, Archie Durkin was at some sort of doctor having his pubic hair analyzed for protein imbalances because both Joyce Slutzky and Yolanda suspected liver dysfunction.

I finished my juice and got up to leave. "There's one other thing you should know," Joyce Slutzky said. "Yolanda is never wrong."

Life only got better. When I returned to my office, Frick Rips told me that my mother had called. Frick Rips was large and doughy. He spoke very softly and he blinked a lot, usually at the same time he said "um." You'd think that with all that going against him, he wouldn't speak too much, but he did. "Um, your mother called," Frick said, "and she, um, forgot to tell you that, um, she included a letter in the package with your, um, laundry."

Because we had free shipping at the show, I used to overnight my dirty laundry to my mother. "Is this really necessary?" my father had said.

"Leo Tolstoy's father sent out his laundry from Russia to Holland on a regular basis," I had said.

Frick went on. "Your mother said she, um, UPS'd the package yesterday so, um, it should be there today. And also, um, the letter was from someone in England called, um, Eugene." Then Frick went out to walk his dog.

If an assistant hadn't come in just then to announce an emergency meeting, I would have been out the door and on the way to getting my hands on the letter from Eugene. Instead, I sat around a conference table with some cast members, production assistants, and the other writers in a room that contained a tank of helium with a nozzle. Talking in a high, squeaky voice amused some of us at *Taped But Proud* to no end, especially late at night.

"Guys, we have exactly seventy-eight hours until the show tapes," Joyce Slutzky said. She looked in a small mirror on the wall and studied her face with the care of a hygienist. She adjusted her hair. I imagined what Eugene had said in his letter. And then I went on to imagine my future with Eugene. Of course, a cozy future with Eugene meant Margaret would have to have a miscarriage, but I could live with that. Okay, go ahead and hate me. Take into account, though, that my daydream allowed for Margaret to go on to marry a charming fellow and have twins (a boy and a girl) and be very happy.

"Yolanda is getting a vibe that the show will be a success," Joyce Slutzky said, "but only if we can come up with one more audience participation segment." Everyone took notes.

One of the writers raised his hand. "Can the idea be conceptual?" he said. I think I speak for the room when I say that nobody understood what he was talking about. Joyce Slutzky thought for a moment before she said, "As long as it's really funny." A few days later, he was fired. He became a photographer known for his abstract studies of weather.

"Okay, writers," Joyce Slutzky said, her eyes on the clock. "I want each of you to have three bulletproof ideas for audience participation. Let's meet back here in exactly one-half hour." She looked at herself once again in the mirror, then applied some lipstick. "And everybody: tomorrow, nine on the dot. That means writers, too!" she said. "The way you guys have been straggling in . . . I swear, if this were Dr. Traub's office, we'd have lost all our patients by now."

Before meeting Archie Durkin, Joyce Slutzky had spent six years working for Dr. Traub, DDS. The experience must have been profound because Joyce Slutzky ran *Taped But Proud* as much like a dentist's office as possible. We might have been the only comedy show in history, for instance, whose staff was encouraged to floss.

I doubt, however, that Dr. Traub had regularly expected his

employees to hang around until two or three in the morning, often doing work that would be thrown away the next day. But no matter how many hours we worked, no matter how many bulletproof ideas we had to concoct, I was in heaven. Please make us work on our day off this week, too, I used to think, though, of course, I piped up in hearty agreement whenever the other writers griped about our sweatshop conditions. Submission to peer group pressure was and remains an operative practice in my life.

Joyce Slutzky, now standing by the door to the conference room, strained her eyes to get a last look at herself before the meeting disbanded. "One more thing," she said, "I can't work in an office without a full-length mirror. Can I get a PA on that? Greta?"

You couldn't ask for a more eager beaver than I. While the other writers lingered in the hall, debating how soon after the electrocution of an actress they could make fun of it in a sketch, I rushed back to my office to get right to work. In no time, I had five ideas for audience participation. The one that was received best was: "How about if one of the cast, maybe Dirk, goes through people's wallets?" But the one of which I was most proud had to do with seating audience members one at a time and then asking them to decide at what point they thought that a few people sitting in chairs became an audience of people sitting in chairs. No one at *Taped But Proud* seemed to get it. At the time, I thought maybe it was too smart for TV, but now I think it was too stupid.

That night, I was racing home to read the letter and there on a street corner not far from the show, you'll never guess who was buying a hot dog from a vendor. My old friend and next-door neighbor, Obax Geeddi. How ecstatic to see her I was! And also rendered shockingly homesick for a stage of my life I had recently thought I hated. The "I don't believe it!"'s and the "Is it really you!?"'s and the girl hugs and the girl yelps went on for a long stretch until it felt right and necessary to stop and ask each other, "What are *you* doing here?"

You, of course, know what I was doing there—trying as hard as I could not to be a big failure in the world of the low-brow. Obax, on the other hand, was working for a human rights organization. I didn't catch the name, but it sounded terrifically worthy. "Father pulled strings in Somalia," she said. "He was afraid if he didn't think of something for me to do I would actually make use of my polar studies background."

I pointed to the swanky fur hat Obax was wearing. "How does that sit with the activists?" I said.

"We're for *human* rights," Obax said. "They don't care how many rabbits you kill."

"Have you heard from Etienne?" I said in the hope Obax would follow up her answer with a question for me about Eugene.

"Etienne who?" Obax said. She laughed. I waited for her to mention Eugene.

"I heard from Eugene," I said finally. "He's leaving Margaret."

"How can that be?" Obax said. "I heard Margaret is pregnant." Obax looked abashed. "Sorry," she said. "Joy told me. I should have told you, but I just couldn't." Obax could have used the excuse that she didn't have my address, but I didn't point that out.

"She had a miscarriage," I said gravely. As long as I was going to lie a little, I might as well lie a lot. "It's so sad," I said. "Tell Joy." Then, I couldn't help grinning.

"And then he left her?" Obax said. "What a creep. You know, you're so lucky he dumped you."

"Actually, he's coming to New York to visit me," I said. "And I'm late."

We traded phone numbers in haste and promised to see each other very soon. The promise was genuine on my part and I sense that it was for Obax, too. "Give Eugene my best," she said as we parted. That sounded less genuine.

I arrived at my apartment around four in the morning, and in the elevator on the way up to my floor, I tore open the carton of clothes, frantically fishing out the letter. It was sandwiched between two items of underwear and I took that as a good omen. I read the letter in the hallway outside my door. It wasn't a letter. It was a birth announcement. Across the top, Eugene had handwritten, "He's a lovely, lovely human being." I calculated that at the time Eugene had made that assessment, his son, Perseus Austen Obello, six and a half pounds at birth, was three weeks old.

I crumpled up the announcement and threw it in the trash. It was five o'clock. How soon, I wondered, could I call Obax to tell her that she had been tragically misinformed by her old friend? On the assumption that human rights start early, I figured an hour. Waiting is what I did next. Waiting is a slow activity.

On the dot of six o'clock, I took the carefully folded scrap of paper with Obax's phone number out of my pocketbook. Only, damn damn damn, what I held in my hand instead was my scrap of paper with my phone number. In the hustle and giddiness, Obax and I had forgotten to make the swap. O fateful twist. For the life of me, I could not track her down, and you better believe every human rights organization was beseeched in the effort.

Three hours later, I was trying to keep my eyes open at the writers' meeting, during which we pitched our bulletproof sketch ideas. It was Frick's turn. "There was, um, a mommy and a daddy and a little girl," he said, "and they all, um, went to Central Park one, um, sunny day." Frick's dog, which was lying by his feet, made a dog sound. "The little girl was, um, thirsty, so the

mommy said, 'I know! Um, let's find a, um, water fountain.' "
Frick looked around the room, as if he had stopped at the really
suspenseful part in order to heighten the tension. " 'Mmm,' said
the little girl after, um, she took a sip of, um, water. 'This water
is, um, good.' 'That's, um, nice,' said the daddy." I closed my eyes
for a little while and when I opened them, I saw another writer
yawn. "The little girl took, um, another sip," Frick said, "and then
a cute, um, doggie came up to the little girl, wagging his tail.
And, then, um"—Frick gave his dog a pat—"the doggie raped
the girl." Frick blinked several times. All other eyes were on
Frick's dog.

You must give Joyce Slutzky credit. "I don't think we could
get a dog to do that," she said.

The next day, my parents came up from Philadelphia to see
a taping of *Taped But Proud*. They brought me a navy blue blazer
because my mother had concluded, after giving my wardrobe
careful thought, that that was the piece, as she said, "to pull
everything together." My parents had also brought me a large
bag of ice because you can always use ice. And they brought my
grandmother.

"Why don't you have anything on the show?" my mother
said.

"The reason I don't have anything on the show," I said with
restrained anger, "is because it is the girlfriend of the producer
who chooses the material and the only thing she seems to like
is smut."

"In that case," my mother said, "it wouldn't kill you to write
a little smut."

"Our mailman says his kids watch the show all the time and
they're very impressed you're one of the writers," my father said.

"You know what I think?" my grandmother said. "I think you
should take a break from this job and go back to get your PhD."

"Anyone can get a PhD, Mother," my father said. "But they say it's almost impossible to get hired at *Taped But Proud*."

My grandmother looked at my father with disbelief. "That's what the mailman says," my father said.

At the taping, my parents and grandmother sat next to Frick's parents, who appeared to be a very courteous couple. Mrs. Rips had gray hair, something no other mother I knew had, thanks to beauty parlors. Mr. Rips had his son's blink. The taping lasted four hours—in other words, four times as long as an actual show. Most of that time was spent shooting retakes of the sketch about leprosy because the director had a problem with the way the actress cried. "Can you try to look less ugly when you cry?" he kept hollering at the actress. This made the actress cry for real and not in a way that was to the director's liking.

Frick had a sketch on the show. In it, a voluptuous lady in a leather bikini stood on a TV news set and spun a giant roulette wheel onto which was strapped a little albino man. Around the circumference of the wheel, in place of numbers, were various weather forecasts. And so, depending on where the albino's head pointed when the wheel came to a stop, the bikinied lady could foretell, for instance, a drop in barometric pressure. The sketch was called "Waste Meat Rain" and Joyce Slutzky's psychic, Yolanda, loved it.

They did the sketch in one take. You could say it was a miracle. God knows what Mr. and Mrs. Rips made of "Waste Meat Rain." My mother thought the lady's leather whip was a gratuitous touch. There was general agreement in both families, according to my father, that the only big problem with the show was that the closing credits went by too fast.

Also in the audience was Corby O'Donnell-McDonald, the actor/lobsterman who had so patiently analyzed every non-nuance with me as I waited for a yes or a no from Archie Durkin. Because no one at *Taped But Proud* seemed to pay a bit of attention to telephone bills, Corby and I had been able to keep on talking with abandon.

"My uncle Walt can't come to the taping because his son was suspended from the eleventh grade for running a craps racket during study hall," I had said to Corby, who'd reversed the charges from Monhegan Island in Maine.

"Inspiring," Corby had said.

"Then my mother asked her friend Janice to go, but Janice's basement flooded; and after that, more catastrophes happened to other people my parents invited," I had said. "So will you go? I have an extra ticket. It's tomorrow."

"Why don't you invite Dwayne Schmokler's attorney-at-law?" Corby had said. It was charming, when you think about it, how much Corby evidently did not want to lay eyes on me.

"Did I mention that there will be models at the party after the show?" I had said. It was Corby's goal to meet a model. Corby, it should be noted, hadn't had a girlfriend for a few years. "Why not start at the top?" he'd said. That sounds more obnoxious now than it did when he said it, I guess because we both knew how pathetic he was, women-wise.

The party after the show was at the new chic place, an innovative steak house called What's at Steak. There was no steak on the menu. That was the innovation. My parents and grandmother sat near the lamb chop station, talking with vigor, no doubt, about me. My grandmother later reported to me that Archie Durkin stopped by their table to tell them that I was doing a super job. That made their night.

I sat with a few of the cast members—the actress who never wanted to be in a sketch unless she could wear period costume décolleté; the former stand-up who, no matter what anyone was talking about, would butt in to say, "I have a bit about that in my act"; and the token fatso actor. Joyce Slutzky strutted over to our table. "Anyone have any gum?" she said. She pointed at me. "I know you don't because I already looked through your purse." I didn't know how to take that, so I ignored it. As soon as Joyce Slutzky walked away, the former stand-up said, "A hygienist who chews gum. I have a bit about that in my act."

Corby never met a model that night, but he stood next to one, a very drunk one. Toward the end of the night, she threw up. "If I had been just one inch closer, I would be covered with model-vomit now," Corby told me as we left What's at Steak. He did not mean, how lucky; he meant that he was sorry he hadn't been one inch closer.

We stood on the street corner, Corby hailing a cab. "I'm going to say something I've never said before," I said. "Look how gorgeous the light is. Something about the way the street-lights are cutting through the night mist."

Corby looked around; I could tell he agreed. "And I'm going to say something I've never said before and never will again," he said. "Isn't it kind of beautiful-looking the way one person is sitting on that bench and one person is sort of reclining?"

"And that old car," I said. "And believe me, never in my life have I ever noticed a car before."

"Okay, I'm going to say something else," Corby said. "I'm not saying that I want to kiss you, or that there were birds up in the trees but I must have never heard them before, or whatever the lyrics of that song are, but, and I've really never said this, this is a very romantic scene."

"Quiet!" a voice boomed. "Annnnnd action!" Corby and I were on the set of a movie, standing not far from the fog machine. The car was a vintage coupe from 1961. The man on the bench was that famous actor, what's-his-name.

"I guess this is a metaphor," Corby said. "But I don't know for what." We got into a cab. He dropped me off at my apartment and continued on to his crappy hotel.

Lucky us at *Taped But Proud*! Asbestos had been detected in the office, so we got the next two days off while it was being taken out. During the break, I slept. On the second day, I was woken up for good by a phone call. "Did I wake you, darling?"

I cleared my throat. Before I had a chance to say anything, even hello, I heard, "It's so lovely to hear your voice."

"Eugene?" I said. Darling? I thought.

"I've got some good news," Eugene said. I braced myself. Good news for one person, I have noticed, is often bad news for another. And by "another," I always mean me.

"Where are you?" I said.

"Princeton has offered me a position," Eugene said. "Isn't that brilliant?" In retrospect, I think what he meant was "Aren't I brilliant?" "I start teaching in a fortnight," Eugene said. "A seminar called 'Toward a Philosophy of the Number Two'; and if that goes well, they said I could have a go at the number three."

"It could be endless," I said.

"Infinite," Eugene said. "And the best part, my loveling, is how near to one another we'll be." He said this with what sounded like sincerity. By now, you might be thinking that Eugene's phone call will turn out to have been a dream, but this is not that kind of a book.

"You're certain I didn't waken you?" Eugene said. It was four in the afternoon.

"I've been up for hours," I said. Then I muffled a yawn. I was happy, but not as happy as one might have thought, which in fact made me feel a tiny bit triumphant.

Oh happy day. It was time to get up and do my laundry.

The next day, Joyce Slutzky called me into her office. The

last time I had been there, she'd shown me her new watch and promised that if I continued to do such excellent work, she would buy me an identical one. She had also said that she was not fond of a particular writer, Victor, because he looked like Abraham Lincoln. Victor did in fact look like the sixteenth president of the United States, but this, in my opinion, was no reason to hate him.

I was expecting something along those lines from Joyce Slutzky. Instead, she pulled her hair into a ponytail and said, "Yolanda told me that you are after Archie." I didn't know what to say. It seemed rude to tell her that Archie wasn't handsome or smart or charming; and it seemed irrelevant to tell her about Eugene. What I said was, "Archie? He never even comes around the office anymore!" Pointing that out, I see now, was not enough to get me off the hook.

"But that's not the reason we're going to have to let you go," Joyce Slutzky said. "Archie and I both feel that you are not giving this job your all."

"I'm not giving it my any," I said. I don't know why I said that. Truth is not, as a rule, where I go to first, but I guess my defenses were down. Joyce Slutzky sat back so fast her ponytail bounced. Convention dictated that I storm off in a huff, but I just sat there, stunned. How would I tell my parents? I wondered. Perhaps I might begin: "Remember how you thought the credits on *Taped But Proud* went by too fast?"

Let me say it again: I was stunned. I'd never been fired before, let alone from the best job in the world. On the positive side, I would no longer have to hate myself whenever I took time off to do something that could have no redeeming satire potential.

Part 3

HIM AGAIN

EIGHT

That's mine!" a naked lady said to me as she clutched a ruffled plaid miniskirt to her chest. "I found it first! It's the last one!" The lady wasn't completely naked. She wore underwear and, hanging off one bra strap, a Velcro shoulder pad. She and I were among a crush of naked women in the dressing room at a sample sale.

I should not have been there. I should have been at work, where I was one of three writers on a children's show called *Tattle TV.* In this show, real children took their grievances to a jury of fake children (child actors) who delivered a verdict as to whether the real children or their parents or their siblings or their teachers were the guilty party, as the case may be, as the case might have been. The show was produced by Frick Rips, which meant it wasn't like other children's shows. For instance, there was a segment called "What Mommy and Daddy Do After You Go to Sleep." The writers did not have a lot to do, but still, a trial concerning an alleged unfair bedtime was pending and I was out of the office, trying on a black lace crop top.

I pulled the top over my head and tried to wriggle into it. "If you're not going to take that, can I try it on?" the naked lady, still holding the ruffled plaid miniskirt, said.

"Sorry," I said, "but I think I am going to buy it." I didn't want the top—it was, I'd say, two sizes too small for me—but I wanted her to have it less. And that is how I came to be wearing the black lace crop top that didn't fit when I saw Eugene for the first time in seven years.

Eugene never did go to Princeton. Long after he was supposed to have started teaching there, my parents forwarded a postcard to me from him. "My dear," he wrote. "Said nay to Princeton. Decided at last minute that the Philosophy of Two (& perhaps Three)—my proposed area of study—overly elitist. Was looking ahead to seeing much of you. Drat! Will be in constant touch. All love, Eugene."

I believed him. I kept the postcard in my pocketbook for months and waited for him to call even after that.

Don't think I didn't go out with other guys during those years. But that isn't this story. And besides, none of the guys is worth telling you about. None had read Zeno in the ancient Greek. None had even read Zeno. None usually had a copy of the Magna Carta in his pocket. None spoke about the joys of reciting poetry while looking out o'er the prow of a boat. None had "learn to play didgeridoo" on his To Do list. None could sing the rules of cricket. None had brown eyes with kind of yellow-specky things. None kissed the way Eugene did, which wasn't that special, I have come to see, but this was before I came to see that. None put salt on his pizza.

If by "constant touch," Eugene meant a couple of Christmas cards in seven years, then he had kept his word. The first was a crayon picture done by Perseus, then one and a half years old, with a list on the back of all the words he could say. They included "Mama," "Dadda," "doggie," "peace," "goodwill," "free will," and "atheist." Several years later, another Christmas greeting came—an audiocassette with a photo of Perseus on the cover and his favorite songs inside. He seemed to favor an Australian aborigine beat. It said a lot about Eugene that he was so ardent about his son, and I guess that was admirable, but I would have appreciated a message that had a little something as well about him and me. Or at least about me.

The next year, I think it was, an item in the Cambridge alumni magazine mentioned that Eugene had won a generous grant to explore "the realm of self-reflection." If I'm remembering this right, he got the grant from the London Society of Ego Studies. (Blame them, if you blame anyone, for the term "ego-ology.") Eugene, Margaret, and Perseus, according to the magazine, had moved to Vienna, where Eugene was being psychoanalyzed by a psychoanalyst who had psychoanalyzed a relative of the Rat Man, who, of course, was psychoanalyzed by Freud. In other words, the top man in the field.

But by that time I didn't care about Eugene. I really didn't. Not in the same way as before. Corby and I were living together in the best of all arrangements—a rent-stabilized illegal sublet with a marooned cable hookup near the elevator that was ours free of charge, courtesy of a long cord. Corby had quit being a lobsterman because it turned out he was allergic to salt water. Plus, he hadn't been meeting any models in Maine or getting any acting work. So he moved to New York to pursue anyone and anything to be had. What he landed in addition to me as his roommate was a job teaching SAT preparation courses to high school students.

One night, as we were watching a late-night infomercial for

a towel on which you could bake a cake at the beach, Corby said, "On occasion, you and I share the same: a) pizza b) bed c) toothbrush d) all of the above?"

"That's a trick question," I said.

"Think again," Corby said. "There are no trick questions on a standardized test."

"You used my toothbrush!" I said. "Ew, ew, ew, ew, ew."

"And not just cakes!" the man on TV, who was wearing a bathing suit, said. "It bakes cookies! Brownies! And even madeleines like the ones made by Marcel Proust!"

"True or false," Corby said. "It is time to change the channel."

"Where were you when I was doing my questionnaires?" I said. The telephone rang and Corby picked it up. There was the usual phatic exchange, then he cupped the phone and said to me, "Is it: a) your mother? b) someone else's mother? Or c) someone so fed up with my shenanigans, he or she just hung up?"

I snatched the phone and said hello.

"It is I," Eugene said.

"Eugene?" I said. I didn't know for sure where my conversation with Eugene would go, so I turned my back on Corby. "Eugene?" I said again, because there was silence on the other end of the line. "Eugene?"

"To hear you utter my name is more melodic to my ears than any concerto," Eugene said. "Can you believe ten years have elapsed since we met?" In point of fact, nine years had elapsed, but I let it lapse.

"It seems we're a stone's throw away from each other, no?" Eugene said.

"I guess so," I said. Surely, I thought, the great intellect I used to know would never have marveled about the magic of the telephone. Or was it some kind of metaphor? I had become either too smart or too dumb for Eugene, I thought.

"Because the truth of it is, my cloudless day, I'm in New York," he said.

Eugene was in town, he went on to say, because he had an appointment, effective immediately, at the Emmerlich Psychoanalytic Institute. He would be teaching a class on the history of the id. "How's that for everything one can need and desire?" Eugene said.

So that you are not as confused as I initially was, I should tell you that over the past few years, Eugene had transformed himself from what he called an "analytic philosopher" to a "philosophic analyst." Why? I think he felt, in a nutshell, that he had answered the fundamental questions of existence, knowledge, and ethics, and that now it was time to move on to the mystery of the mind.

"This is a bad connection," I said. There was nothing wrong with the connection. "Can we talk tomorrow?" I had the feeling Corby was still watching me.

"I would positively like that, my one," Eugene said. "It would be better if I called you. Margaret is flying in tonight to look for a flat."

I gave Eugene my number at *Tattle TV* and hung up. "My crazy cousin," I said to Corby and rolled my eyes. "In and out of asylums. It's sad, actually."

" 'Sobriquet' is to 'given name' as 'crazy cousin' is to what?" Corby said.

"Leave me alone," I said. "I already got into college."

Did Eugene call the next day? No, he did not. Nor the next day. A week later, while Frick Rips was in my office, put out because the network censors had banned his firearms and children segment, the telephone rang. "Excuse me," I said to Frick, muting the phone when I heard Eugene's voice. "I have to take this. It's my crazy cousin. There's a problem with his Lithium."

"Um, awesome," said Frick.

On the phone, Eugene told me about Perseus's reading level (on par with a fourteen-year-old's though he was only seven!) and the cute way Perseus pronounced "Heraclitus of Ephesus," but Eugene did not tell me why he hadn't called when he said he would. And you know me well enough to know I would never ask.

Not only that. When Eugene asked me to meet him for a drink that night, I did not hesitate to say yes even though—wouldn't you know?—I was wearing my madras shirt from high school.

So off I went to the sample sale, mumbling something to Frick Rips about a ledge emergency with my crazy cousin; and from there, wearing my new black lace crop top, to the loft belonging to Eugene's college friend who had become a famous magician. The magician was on tour, leaving his keys and his graffiti art and his video games all to Eugene.

Eugene answered the door in running shorts and a rugby shirt. The magician had a home gym. The madras shirt would have been fine, I thought. "Persuasive top," Eugene said. Maybe the madras shirt wouldn't have been so fine after all—too unpersuasive.

"Where's Margaret?" I said. Wouldn't you think I'd have said something along the lines of "Wow! It's been too long!" I did not say this because wouldn't you think Eugene would have said the same thing? I'm good at picking up cues. Too good.

"She and Percy flew off to England this morning," Eugene said. "May I offer you some wine? It's an eighty-two Lafite."

I raised my eyebrows. "Eighty-two?" I said, hoping to sound as if eighty-two meant something different to me than eighty-three. "That would be delicious." As soon as the words came out of my mouth, I had doubts that "delicious" was a wine term, but I couldn't unsay it. At least I had the sophistication not to say 1982; at least I knew Eugene had been talking about this century.

Eugene and I sat not too close together on the suede sectional sofa, drinking our '82 Lafite. A sword, presumably for swallowing, hung on the wall opposite. I'm not trying to be cute and symbolic; that's just the way it was. Previous to that night, the most alcohol I had ever drunk in one sitting was a fraction of a glass. That night the record was broken handily. This is only to say that I had had about two glasses. That would translate to about twenty glasses for a normal person like you. "Is it okay to put my glass on this without a coaster?" I said.

"That's a logical fallacy," Eugene said, "since you have already dropped the glass and spilled the wine." Eugene and I laughed. "Besides," he said, "women within the confines of that *objet* have been sawed in two." Oh, how we laughed. Again.

Eugene asked me about my job at *Tattle TV* and because I was too nervous and too tipsy, there was no way I could manage omitting a single detail. "So then we have this segment, 'The Time-Out Electric Chair,' that I'm in charge of," I said. "Well, not in charge of. I produce it with another writer, Valentine Siracuse. Isn't Valentine Siracuse a funny name?"

As I jabbered on, Eugene stretched out on his section and a little of my section, too, of the sectional sofa. He looked at me intently and made a beckoning gesture with his forefinger. "Come here," Eugene said. I did.

"You mean to tell me you're thirty years old and an inane man tells you to 'come here,' and just like that, you *do*!" my father might have said. To which I might have said, "Nobody told me I had a choice. And besides, he was looking extremely attractive at that very moment."

Just talking about this embarrasses me.

"You would like Valentine," I said to Eugene at top speed. "He's from Fredonia—were you even aware there was a Fredonia? I wasn't." Eugene, I knew full well, wasn't paying attention. He was kissing my neck. I kept on talking, under the assumption that if I stopped in the middle of my story, if you can even call it a story, then Eugene would know that I knew he wasn't listening and then he would feel hurt. "It's like Transylvania," I said. "I didn't know until, like a few years ago, that there was really such a place. Anyway, what I'm supposed to be working on right now is a segment about unfair bedtime."

Eugene looked up at me. "Speaking of bedtime . . ." he said.

"Yes," I said with gusto, grateful for the opportunity to keep talking. "It's a pretty interesting case. Rachel Lewis versus the parents of Rachel Lewis. Rachel argues that—"

"Hush, my Desdemona," said Eugene. So much for keeping up my end of the conversation.

He means Juliet, I thought with cheer. Then I remembered, Either way, I end up dead.

Eugene kissed me on the mouth. He led me into the bedroom. In this bedroom, there was, instead of a bed, a coffin as wide as a king-size mattress. There was also a love seat with spikes on the seat; a shackle escape contraption hanging from a hook on the door; photographs of circus freaks on the wall; and muted purple light. Get the picture? In this context, one could imagine that the rabbit rug in front of the fireplace was sewn from rabbits pulled out of the top hat, then zapped with a magic wand to their deaths. The fireplace, by the way, stored fire-related magic tricks, not logs. *This* was not a bedroom; *this* was a bedchamber.

Eugene and I never made it to the coffin. We rolled around on the rabbit rug. Maybe there really was some hocus-pocus going on because when I looked at Eugene, it seemed as if everything about him had shrunk. I'm not saying I was no longer enthralled, because I was. I'm just saying I remembered things differently the first time I'd seen him without clothes. Sorry to be so coy.

When we were done doing things, Eugene squeezed my hand and said, "If you'd like, you can spend the night." This was not the Eugene I used to know.

"Thank you," I said, "but I should get home. I have work to do." What I meant was, "It's only midnight. Lots of my friends are still awake. I have to get on the phone and tell everyone everything."

I put my black crop top back on and left. On the way out, I tripped over a levitation device. On the bus back to my apartment, I rehashed every delirious detail. I was in a daze. I had just slept with the person I lost my virginity to. I love gossip, especially gossip about myself.

Do you want to know what all my friends had to say about me? Did you even know I had friends in New York? You should thank your lucky stars—trust me on this—that I left some parts of my story out. Too large a dose of me, I worry, can be lethal. But anyway, here was the chitchat regarding me:

Lisa: "Can I be honest? Something's wrong with you."

Deb: "If you're happy, I'm happy. You shouldn't be happy, though."

Meg: "I've heard worse, but not much worse."

Joan: "I hope you won't take this the wrong way, but it's clear that Eugene is gay."

Pearson: "The winner in this story is Margaret. She got a night off from him."

Susan: "I'm not saying Eugene's going to throw a Scotch tape dispenser at you someday or that you're going to have to take out a restraining order on him, but it's really weird because Robert also plied me with eighty-two Lafite when we were courting."

Phil: "I like the sound of that black lace crop top."

Buffy: "If I were a better person, this story would turn me into a feminist."

Cynthia: "Does this mean you lost your virginity twice?"

Larry: "How come he can get away with being a sleazeball and I can't?"

Mark: "How, um, big is it anyway?"

Jeff: "What kind of a guy would wear a rugby shirt?"

Martha: "Let me get this straight. You haven't seen the guy for seven years and the first thing he says is 'persuasive'?"

Sarah: "He actually said that? Because if I'm not mistaken, that is a line from a Sinatra song."

Phoebe: "Remind me again why you like him? Is it because he's using you or because he lies to you repeatedly?"

Nina: "You could so easily blackmail that guy."

Ann: "Extremely romantic, but tell me again who Eugene is."

Esther: "Do you think Eugene could find out how to do that trick where you pull a quarter out of someone's ear?"

When I got back to the apartment, Corby was not there. Do you know I actually said to myself, and I mean out loud, "Is Corby a) with a model? b) giving a tutorial in quadratic equations to a twelfth grader? c) bowling? d) dead on the street?" The trick to multiple choice, Corby had taught me, lay in not going for the correct answer but rather eliminating the wrong answers. Bowling seemed unlikely but you never know.

Corby never came home that night.

The next day at work, an intern at the show, Pnicke (pronounced Nicky), aged fifteen, Rollerbladed into my office to tell me that there was an emergency meeting in the head writer's office. The meeting she referred to had taken place an hour before. Pnike was a pothead. Her father was the head of the network. "Also, there's a package or something for you," she said.

Had Eugene sent me flowers? Couldn't a girl dream?

On my way to the mailroom, I ran into Frick Rips in the elevator. He told me that the show had scored in the negative numbers. That's what the meeting had been about. "But it's, um, okay," Frick said. "We don't have to pay anybody any money or, um, anything."

Frick Rips had a way to save the show. His idea was to produce reenactments of real trials; real trials that kids could relate to. "What if we start with a trial that's about, um, a kid?" Frick said.

"That's not bad," I said, not lying. If Eugene spent $100 on a combination of red and white roses, I wondered, and red roses cost twice as much as white roses, how many flowers did Eugene send me?

"I was, um, thinking," Frick said, "that it might be lots of, um, fun to do the, um, the Leopold and Loeb case." He rubbed his hands together the way you would if you were a witch about to boil somebody.

"Leopold and Loeb?" I said. "The one where those college kids killed a fourteen-year-old!"

"Yes," Frick said. "I know our, um, demographic is eight to twelve, but studies show viewers like to, um, identify with older kids."

"I'd watch that," said an old man with what appeared to be earnest enthusiasm as he stepped off the elevator. Viewer studies, it seems, do not always get it right. Frick looked very happy and I was happy for him.

A callow-looking young man with horn-rimmed glasses got on the elevator. He smiled at me and I smiled back. Frick nudged me. "Spitting image," he said, "of, um, Nathan Leopold."

By the next floor, I was sure that Corby was dead, murdered by the twelfth grader he'd been tutoring in quadratic equations. But that would mean the answer was both b) and d). On the mezzanine floor, I thought, Both b) and d)? That cannot be. As Corby had said, the SAT has no trick questions.

When the mailroom guy gave me a knowing look, I knew. My package was not from Eugene. My package was from my mother. My weekly shipment of clean laundry. In this particular carton, my mother had also put in a bunch of my old clothes she thought I might need, including another madras shirt.

I got home that night and Corby was there. Seeing him stuff a slice of pizza into his mouth with such vim, I thought, How dare you be alive after all that worrying I did about your being dead? It wouldn't have gotten me anywhere, of course, to say, "Couldn't you have at least called, you inconsiderate boob?" Therefore, I went with, "Did you put a new roll of toilet paper in the whatever-it's-called as I asked you to do?"

"You can rely on me," Corby said. "I sure did."

"Really?" I said. "Because only an inconsiderate boob puts in the roll so it rolls from the bottom."

"I got fired today," Corby said.

"Shit. Fired. I hate being fired," I said. Then I threw a peach at Corby. It was something we did, throwing fruit at each other. There were rules spelling out how far away the Thrower must be from the Target Person as well as a point system, all too elaborate to go into. The most points you could get came from throwing a watermelon from a distance of ten feet.

The peach hit the wall. "Three points, me," said Corby.

"They didn't find out about your predicate nominative problem, did they?" I said.

"Remember that girl I told you about?" Corby said, rummaging through the fruit bowl.

"The one whose boyfriend convinced her she'd get an eight hundred on her verbal SAT if she stuck cinnamon chewing gum on the upper left-hand corner of her answer sheet?" I said.

"No," Corby said, "that's Kimberly." Corby held up a tomato. "I promise I won't ask ever again. Does this count?"

"The one who, when you asked her to use 'feasible' in a sentence, said, 'My hair isn't feasible today'?" I said. "And yes, tomatoes are fruit."

"The feasible girl is Tiffany," Corby said.

"You don't mean the smart one then?" I said.

"There are no smart ones," Corby said. He wound up for the pitch.

"Ohhhh," I said. "I know who you mean." The tomato hit my ankle. "Ow. Four points, you. You mean the girl who looks like a model."

"Yes. She," said Corby. "And it's *whom* you mean, not *who*, and five not four points because you said 'ow.' "

"Nice try, but you only get extra points for interjections that have four or more letters," I said. "It would be five if I'd said 'ouch.' " Corby stuck his tongue out at me.

"Real mature," I said and then I threw a kiwi at Corby. The kiwi skimmed his hair for two points. "Isn't she the one whose parents are thinking of moving to Idaho so she'll have a better chance of getting into a good college?" I opened the freezer and took out some sorbet.

"Iowa," Corby said. "Hey, sorbet doesn't count. It's a fruit derivative."

"I was going to eat it," I said. "Every once in a while I do that with food."

"Can you believe they fired me?" Corby said.

"What'd you do to deserve it?" I said.

"That's the point," Corby said with indignation. "I didn't do anything. But try telling that to parents when you're lying in bed with their daughter, who is not only naked, but also seventeen years old."

"Corby, what were you thinking?" I said.

"I was thinking that they were spending the weekend at their beach house," Corby said. "Is it my fault Mr. Penney forgot his briefcase in New York?"

"The nerve!" I said.

"I know!" said Corby. "What's their big complaint, anyway? It's not as if I didn't boost Nicky's practice tests almost two hundred points," Corby said.

"Pnicke?" I said. "With a *P?*"

"*N-I-C-K-Y,*" Corby said, giving me a look.

"You'd be surprised," I said.

"Hey, wait," Corby said. "What happened with Eugene last night?"

I shrugged.

"What an asshole," Corby said.

I threw the sorbet at Corby for the hell of it. Got him in the head!

The next day at work, there was no Xerox machine and the day after, no filing cabinets. Every morning, at least one more piece of office equipment was gone and a lot of stationery supplies, too. Before long, *Tattle TV* was without a coffeemaker, a bulletin board, chair mats, staple removers, and reception-area furniture. At first, I'm sorry to admit, we did suspect Nathan Barnhouse. You would have, too. It wasn't only that we had seen him pocket powdered creamer packets off the snack wagon. He looked like the thief type.

Then, one day, during a production meeting about props for the segment on latchkey kids, a couple of men from janitorial carried out the conference table. "Excuse, um, me," Frick Rips said, "but we were, um, using that to, um, put our things on."

"Sorry," one of the men said. "They said take it away." "They" were the vice presidents in programming. In the days to come, it became clear that rather than cancel our show, the network was taking it away, pencil by pencil. The last week *Tattle TV* was in operation, we worked in pitch blackness. Janitorial had removed the fluorescent tubing from the light fixtures.

Suddenly, everyone was sucking up to Pnicke, in the hope that her head-of-the-network father had some jobs to hand out—everyone except Frick Rips, who stayed in his office, making jewelry out of cockroaches he had shellacked when we still had overhead lights.

Meanwhile, Eugene. Can you believe he never called? After there was nothing left of *Tattle TV,* not even a three-hole punch, I tried to reach him. The phones in the office had been disconnected and I was afraid Eugene might not know where to find me. That he wasn't looking was a choice I preferred not to consider. I called the magician's loft. The magician answered. The magician had cut short his national tour after his dove flew out of a top hat and took a bite out of the magician's thumb. "I don't know if I'll ever be able to trust a dove again," the magician said.

"Doves," I said with the weariness of one who had been betrayed by doves oh-so-many times. The magician told me Eugene had disappeared. "Poof!" he said. I pictured Eugene getting smaller and smaller until he was nothing. He should have called. He owed me that. Surely Eugene, professor of the id, could understand that.

What crossed my mind was that maybe Corby had been right about Eugene. Maybe Eugene was an asshole. I kept that opinion to myself, but it's okay if you know.

The next day, a box of jumbo Maryland blue crabs on ice came from my parents. Nestled under a claw was a postcard from Eugene. "The other night," the card said, "was—dare I say?—magical. Had to rush back to England thereafter because Margaret is hyperglycemic. Oh, my! Hugs, Eugene."

"Eugene was hit by a bus," I said to Corby, who was smashing a crab flat with a footstool. "Fractures, internal bleeding, the works." I paused to shudder ostentatiously. "That's why he never showed up or called. They airlifted him to England."

Corby did not look convinced. He whacked another crab. I took up a cast-iron skillet and joined the whacking until the charm of the project had worn off.

"Eugene wasn't really hit by a bus, was he?" Corby said, sitting on the footstool.

I threw some shards of crab into the trash and then I said, "No, he might just be an asshole." If Eugene had been hit by a bus, I thought, he would have called it an "autobus."

NINE

Whenever anyone asked Corby what he was doing to make money since he was no longer in SATs, he said he had a job killing dogs for the city. That shut everyone up, everyone except our next-door neighbor. She wanted to know what kind of dogs.

"It would take the wind out of you," Corby told me he had said to her, "if I told you how many Dalmatian owners want to put their Dalmatian puppies to sleep simply because the spots aren't in the right place." From then on, our next-door neighbor picked up her little dog whenever Corby was around, even though the dog had no spots. Did I ever tell you about that dog of hers? He growled at anyone who carried two of anything. The dog could handle one bag or many bags, for instance, but two bags, he went nuts.

Now that I'm telling you this, I'm wondering if Eugene had been on to something with his proposal to study the philosophy of two. And to give credit where credit is due, could the dog also have been on to something?

Anyway, what Corby was in fact doing was taking in-line skating lessons. After his Nicky misadventure, I'd introduced Corby to Pnicke. He decided that the only way to woo Pnicke, who lived in her Rollerblades, was to share her obsession.

While Corby was learning how to brake on a hill, I was misusing my time in a different way.

After I'd lost my job at *Tattle TV,* my parents, assuming I was as distraught as they were, sent me a check for therapy. Accordingly, I spent my days at the Diana Adorian Salon undergoing restorative pedicures; rehabilitative manicures; remedial neck rubs, Japanese-style; skin-renewing facials, French-style; reconstructive hair work; rejuvenating body peels; hydrotherapy; aromatherapy; thermotherapy; mud therapy; paper, rock, and scissors therapy; salt exfoliation treatments; fresh pepper purges; massages with biointrinsic herbs and essential oils; toxin-draining body wraps; and some other cures. (Note: I did not sign up for a leech drainage, though it was listed in the brochure.)

"So?" my father said on the phone the day after my first appointment at the salon. "Have you changed?"

"Nooohhww," I said in the same adorable manner a sullen teenager might answer the question "Were you smoking marijuana up in your room last night?" I rolled my eyes, even though I was alone. I coulda been a method actor. Come to think of it, we all coulda been and maybe even are.

"Jesus Christ," my father said. "When do you think you will change?" The facialist had said I could expect to see results in four to six weeks, but I didn't share that with my father.

I sighed loudly. "Therapy wasn't my idea," I said.

"Nor mine," my father said.

I looked down at my vitamin A—enriched nails and noticed that a polish touch-up was in order. Was there time to squeeze in an appointment after I picked up my unemployment check?

"But I am making definite progress," I said. "So thanks, Daddy."

By this time, I trust there's no need to tell you why I was dolling myself up. He had finally called. He had wanted to call sooner, he said, but had been tied up with teaching and house hunting and Perseus's school project on the wampum jewelry of the Shinnecock Indian Nation. On top of that, he had given a presentation to the Reality Club on the topic "Why does our 'humanness' keep getting in the way of rational decision-making?"

"I'd really like to see you," he had said without a trace of the English accent he'd had in England and even the last time I saw him. "There were parts of your body I neglected last time. When can we meet?"

"I'm free today," I said.

"Today I have . . . today's not promising," Eugene said.

"Let me look at my appointment book," I said.

Cut to: sound effects of opening a drawer, ransacking contents of drawer, closing drawer, shuffling through take-out menus that had been lying around on counter.

"Actually, tomorrow I'm free and the next day and, let me check . . ." I allowed for checking time, and then said perhaps too happily: "All my days look pretty good."

"Days are dicey," Eugene said.

"Nights are good, too," I said, full steam ahead.

"Nights," Eugene said. "Nights are bad."

"I seem to be free every day until, let's see . . . April, free; May, free; June, free; free, free, free, free until . . . Thanksgiving," I said. "I'm busy Thanksgiving. And I see here that it's really only the night of Thanksgiving I can't do, and even then, my family eats fast."

"Are you playing hard to get?" Eugene said. It was a joke but nevertheless stung. Did he not understand that I was joking, too? "Can you do coffee a week Tuesday?" he said. "My last class lets out at six thirty-five."

By 5:35 Tuesday, the roadwork on my body had been completed, including a nail polish touch-up, all courtesy of Diana Adorian. I sat on a stool in the kitchen, waiting at attention, too groomed to risk moving a muscle. The phone rang. I figured, and I bet you did, too, that it was Eugene calling to cancel.

"This is Dr. Hut," a man said, presumably Dr. Hut. The tone was sober. It smacked of negative lab reports, something wrong with the biopsy, enlarged spleen, protein deficiencies, high white cell blood count, glucose level not within normal range, don't like the look of that node, suspicious spot, organ failing, arteries iffy, metastasized something, irregular everything, functions malfunctioning, numbers not good, have you always had that, not a good sign, may I be blunt, six months tops.

Dr. Hut's name rang no bell and as far as I knew, I hadn't had a medical test in years. But you could never be absolutely sure about what those ladies in lab coats at Diana Adorian were really up to. Dr. Hut could have gotten word of my condition from one of them.

"I never met you, so it can't be bad news," I said, letting Dr. Hut in on my thought process.

"Correct," Dr. Hut said, "inasmuch as it is not bad news about you." He cleared his throat. Clearing throats, never good. "However, inasmuch as you are the person the patient designated as a contact, you may not deem the news auspicious," he said.

"You are quite correct, though, in your assumption that no news is as sad as sad news about oneself," Dr. Hut said. He had taken me from confusion to concern and dropped me off at plain annoyance.

"What is this about?" I said.

"It is Cornelius O'Donnell-McDonald I'm calling about," Dr. Hut said.

"Corby?" I said.

Dr. Hut told me that Corby had fallen during a skating lesson and broken his leg. "Technically, a Lisfranc fracture," Dr. Hut said. "Fewer than one percent of all foot fractures occur in the tarsometatarsal joint, so this is highly unusual." Dr. Hut sounded highly pleased to have such a highly unusual case. "It is even more highly unusual because it occurred in a foot supported by a stiff boot case," he said, evidently bursting with high delight at that bonus fact.

Okay, so Corby had broken his leg; sooner or later, everyone breaks something. I'm not being callous. It's just that, well, bones heal. Still, I guess I should have been thinking about Corby's suffering. Instead, I was wondering if I would have time for coffee with Eugene before picking Corby up. But how to put the question delicately? "Dr. Hut," I said, "how long does it take plaster of paris to dry?"

"Pardon?" Dr. Hut said.

"Nothing," I said, trying to think of what to say next. "I was just hoping he can still take his trip to Paris and fly . . . there."

"The patient is in the recovery room now," Dr. Hut said, never acknowledging the idiotic thing I had just said. "How soon do you think you could get here?" That was that.

Before leaving for the emergency room, I called Eugene to reschedule. "A Lisfranc fracture?" Eugene said on the phone. "Might you mean the one named after the field surgeon in Napoléon's army?"

"It's highly unusual," I said. "That's all I can tell you."

"The original injury Lisfranc described came about when a soldier fell off his horse, but his foot remained in the stirrup, or so the story goes," Eugene said.

"How weird," I said, "to have a fracture named after you. That would be weird, don't you think?"

"In point of fact, Lisfranc is better known for something else," Eugene said.

"What?" I said. "A blister?"

"No," Eugene said. "Would that it were, innocent mine." He paused. "I think I best not tell you."

"Oh, come on. Tell me."

"How keen are you about this friend, if I may be so bold to inquire?" Eugene said in a tone that I took to be either foreboding or flirtatious.

"What?" I said, alarmed but also flattered. "Tell me." At that point, I was definitely being coquettish.

Eugene took a breath. "Okay," he said. "In his day, Jacques Lisfranc was renowned for his ability to amputate a foot in less than one minute using a technique he invented of cutting through the Lisfranc joint."

"Yuck," I said.

"The technique is still used today, sweet pea," Eugene said. Didn't I tell you he was smart? "I'm so sorry I won't be seeing you tonight. But at least I got to spend the day in anticipation." He was romantic, too.

Corby's cast went all the way to the top. As I helped him into a taxi outside the hospital he said, "If I didn't know you, I'd ask you out." I leaned across Corby in order to close the door. "It was a compliment," he said.

"I'd like to point out," I said, "that it could also be the opposite."

"Oh, did I say 'compliment'?" Corby said. "I meant 'adding insult to injury.' " The taxi jerked around a curve and Corby winced.

Since our apartment was a fifth-floor walk-up, Corby moved to his parents' split-level. The morning after the night Corby left, the telephone rang. Eugene called at precisely the time he said he would and I was touched. In my experience, when unreliable people keep promises, it is extra impressive.

"How are you?" I said.

"Depressed," Eugene said. "Someone in the department has published a brilliant piece in the *Journal of Id Studies* linking the growth of technology in post-industrialist society with the end of monogamy."

"How do you like that?" I said, clueless why such news could be thought depressing. Who could be unhappy about the growth of invention? Luggage-on-wheels wasn't yet around, but there was plenty else I personally couldn't live without. The end of monogamy couldn't be getting him down, could it? Because the end of monogamy was something I personally would applaud. I didn't ask Eugene for clarification because what if the answer was obvious?

"I worked on that idea for a year," he said. "Can you believe I considered this man a colleague!" Eugene seemed indignant. "They stab you in the back in academia."

"So they say," I said.

"The maddening part," Eugene said, "is that his take is so simplistic."

"It certainly sounds it," I said.

"I feel much less depressed talking to you," Eugene said. "Can I come over for a hug?"

Eugene did come over. He brought me the notes for his unpublished piece on the sexual ramifications of the affordable car and also a copy of one of his favorite books, *The Viscount of Counterfeit,* which seemed to be about an art forger. Eugene had inscribed the book "Truly and forever, Eugene." This was the only present Eugene had ever given me and I cherished it yet at the same time, saw the fallacy.

We ended up in bed until he had to leave for a one o'clock seminar on prolapsed penis envy. We made a bad joke about the subject, but for your sake and mine and even for Eugene's sake, I won't repeat it. Eugene got dressed, showed me some photos of Perseus from a school play, and kissed me good-bye. As he walked out the door to my bedroom, he turned and said, "You have beautiful coloring."

Margaret's name never came up that morning, nor did it come up at any of our other mornings. Eugene told the people at the Emmerlich Psychoanalytic Institute that he was seeing his psychoanalyst, or that's what Eugene told me he told them, and about that, I had no reason to think he was lying. Maybe you do, but I didn't.

Eugene stayed for roughly fifty minutes, a full session. There was so much I wanted to know. Did he still love Margaret? Did she know about me? Was there anything, in fact, to know? Whose coloring did Eugene like better—Margaret's or mine?

On morning number three, we had croissants and orange juice in my kitchen and Eugene said, "What am I going to do with you?"

If anyone ever says that to you, don't presuppose that the question means the person is trying to figure out how to ditch his wife, get partial custody of his eight-year-old, and still keep the flat in England.

"What are your options?" I said with good cheer.

"I want to make sure you don't get hurt," Eugene said.

"Me? Hurt?" I said. "First of all, I don't get hurt. I would never get hurt. Hurt is not something I do. No siree, not I." I stopped what I was saying to watch Eugene blot up croissant crumbs on his lap with his pinkie. The sight of that or maybe it was something else made me forget second of all.

"And yet, I find your vulnerability enthralling," Eugene said as he blotted up a crumb that had fallen from his pants to the chair.

"Second of all," I said, suddenly remembering second of all, "even if I did get hurt, which I don't, you already hurt me once, so I can't get hurt another time. I'm immunized. You don't have to worry about me. You really, really don't. No, indeed, no."

Ever so delicately, Eugene transported the crumbs on his pinkie up to his mouth and deposited them on his tongue. "I'm not so sure," Eugene said, "but if you say so." Then he asked me if he could have the last croissant.

It was that day, I think, that I had lunch with Obax, who'd located me by calling my parents. This was a farewell lunch because Obax had come to the conclusion that human rights was not for her. She was returning to Somalia to do what she'd always wanted to do: open a *crêperie* in Mogadishu. In light of the famine there, this did not seem like a shrewd idea to me, but Obax reminded me that her father owned a sorghum-processing plant, so she would always have a reliable supply of wheat-flour substitute.

"It would be kind of rude and tacky of me to ask Eugene what's going on with us, wouldn't it?" I said to Obax.

"Are you joking? Even fucking Miss Manners would ask him," Obax said.

"No. I can't," I said, "because then he'll think I'm stupid."

"I'm not sure I follow," Obax said, "but in your defense, I can tell you that in some magazine article or something I read at the hairdresser's, the writer proved that for many men, stupidity is a turn-on." She had certainly learned a lot in New York working for human rights.

"Here's the thing," I said. "Either he can't stand Margaret's coloring and that's why he's seeing me, or he loves Margaret and her coloring and the reason he's seeing me has nothing to do with love. It's one of the two and I don't want him to know I can't figure out which."

"That really *is* stupid," Obax said, fondly resting her hand on my arm, "but I guess I'm not one to talk." Obax's father was backing her on the *crêperie* if and only if she agreed to an arranged marriage.

"I can't believe you still know him," Obax said. "He's a cad and a bore and a sneak and a fake and a narcissist and a braggart and I don't like his teeth, either."

"I'm sure you're right," I said, "but that's just one side of him."

"What about the married thing?" Obax said. "Don't you feel a little bad for Margaret?"

"What does she have to do with it?" I said, and I meant it. I had met Eugene a long time before Margaret had. "Besides," I said, "he seems to really like me this time. And, he's so smart. Being with him is getting an A."

"Yeah, yeah, yeah," Obax said. She'd heard it before. Everyone had, including, well, you, for starters. "As Libby used to say, everyone's smart. Libby was sure smart, wasn't she?" The memory of my last encounter with Libby—when she'd accused me of accusing her of stealing my plaid poncho—surfaced and sunk the merry mental boat I'd been on.

"Do you think your fiancé is smart?" I said. Today, the answer to that question would be, "There are many different kinds of intelligence," but then, we didn't know that. We weren't that kind of smart, I guess.

"Is he called my fiancé if I've never met him?" Obax said. "By the way, you look better than I've ever seen you look."

"Therapy," I said.

Morning number seven, Eugene asked me to have dinner with him. Margaret's father wasn't feeling well—apparently it ran in the family—so Margaret was going to spend the night in Ventnor with her parents. She was taking Perseus.

During the fish course, Eugene held my hand.

That was all it took. "Do you want to sleep over?" I said.

"Where would you sleep?" Eugene said. If I was not understanding something, I guess it was something big. Didn't those mornings count for anything?

"I guess I could sleep in Corby's room," I said. "He's not coming back until tomorrow. He got a walking cast today."

"Is he walking back?" Eugene said.

I no longer knew what was a joke and what wasn't. I gave my famous indecisive grunt.

"Maybe another time," Eugene said. "I have to get up early tomorrow to give a lecture on erotic transference."

That really took the cake. I'm not saying this was the first time someone had turned me down, but always before it was because the guy wanted to do it with someone else, not just theorize to a group of undergrads on the theme of doing it. Talk about feeling snubbed (or, as I accidentally typed at first—snub bed).

But during the cheese course, Eugene said, "I think I will sleep over."

"We could prepare for your erotic transference lecture," I said.

During our walk home, Eugene put his arm around me without even checking first to see if anyone he and Margaret knew was nearby. Things like that have an effect on me. "I am wondering how this all began," he said.

"Not me," I said. "I am wondering how it will end."

"Curious," he said. We stopped at a traffic light and Eugene's hand, which had rested seconds before on my shoulder, went back in his pocket. "In psychoanalysis, we call it termination and it comes about when the patient feels ready to relinquish his or her attachment to the analyst in favor of the pursuit of life." Eugene leaned in and smiled slyly. "But who is the patient here and who is the analyst?"

On the steps to my apartment, we ran into my next-door neighbor, catching her breath at the third-floor landing. Eugene offered to carry her groceries, and judging by her smile, she was thinking about what a gentleman he was compared with that delinquent roommate of mine who killed dogs for the city.

As soon as we walked into my apartment, Eugene handed me his coat and said, "Did you ever see the film *The Incredible Amazing Stupendous Thing*?"

Like, when I was ten, I thought, remembering how excruciatingly bad I thought it had been—and those were the days I was thrilled with any movie so long as it was in color. Detecting a sparkle in Eugene's eyes, though, made me not say that. I told Eugene I'd never seen the movie, but heard it was charming.

"Charming?" Eugene said.

"Well, no. Not charming," I said. "Not exactly charming."

"*The Incredible Amazing Stupendous Thing* is so much more than charming," Eugene said.

Now I get it, I thought. *The Incredible Amazing Stupendous Thing* is a telling metaphor or a dark allegory or a parable for our time or a postmodern fable or a Jungian myth or a haunting tale of magic realism or it has something to do with deconstruction. "So much more," I said.

"*The Incredible Amazing Stupendous Thing* is utterly enchanting," Eugene said. He had seen the movie on television only a few days earlier. "A lot of people think it's for children, and I suppose children would be amused, but really, it's just a very intelligent romp," he said. Then he took off his shirt.

You might think that seeing Eugene the Intellectual in this light would have presented an obstacle to erotic transference. But it didn't. As he left that morning, Eugene said, "You look like a nonlimestone reproduction of the Cretan sculpture 'Lady of Auxerre.' " Of course I probably didn't, but it was nice to hear. Or was it? Remind me to look that up.

A few weeks later, after Corby had gotten his walking cast, he, Eugene, and I took a walk in Central Park. "Don't embarrass me by saying anything dumb," I said to Corby before Eugene arrived.

"What do I look like?" Corby said. "Somebody's parent?" He finished off a clementine and threw the rind at my head.

"Throwing a fruit by-product," I said. "That's a penalty."

During our picturesque walk, Eugene almost got run over by a crazy-looking car that swerved out of the way just in time. "Go back where you came from!" Corby yelled after the car as it careered away. "To *The Incredible Amazing Stupendous Thing* land!" Corby turned to Eugene and me. "Doesn't that car look like the contraption from outer space in that dopey movie?"

"You mean you don't venerate *The Incredible Amazing Stupendous Thing*?" Eugene said.

"Oh, sure," Corby said. "Almost as much *Dr. Doolittle.*" I discreetly kicked Corby's walking cast.

"Ow," Corby said.

"You think of *The Incredible Amazing Stupendous Thing* as a kids' movie?" I said to Corby, feigning incredulity.

"You gotta be kidding," Corby said.

"That movie is utterly charming," I said, taking a gamble Eugene would never remember our conversation. "When you think of it, it's an intelligent and sophisticated romp." I looked at Eugene to see if I'd gotten the recitation right. He seemed pleased.

Corby scrunched up his face as if a little boy. "You're kidding," he said. To Eugene, he said, "You only went because you took Prometheus, right? Your son, right?"

I don't think Eugene heard that. Anyway, he didn't seem to react.

"Maybe you should see the movie from an adult perspective," I said.

"That would be difficult," Corby said. "Maybe we should get a taxi. There's only so much walking you can ask from a guy with a walking cast."

Corby and I dropped Eugene off at his apartment. Margaret's father had died a few days earlier and Eugene was taking care of Perseus while Margaret was with her mother. "Shouldn't you be at the funeral?" I had said to Eugene on our walk. "As her, you know, date?"

"Perhaps," Eugene had said. "But I don't much care for funerals." Eugene had introduced the news about Margaret's father into the conversation by letting me know that his schedule was going to free up presently.

In the taxi, Corby had a conversation with the driver about traffic patterns and Eugene said to me, "It occurs to me that you might want to send Margaret a condolence note."

"Is that really a good idea?" I said. "Letting her know I know her father died?"

"She knows her father died," Eugene said. He chortled.

"I know," I said, "but . . . and I'm not saying that she has anything to be suspicious of . . ."

"She knows that, too," Eugene said. "I've told her that you and I talk. I don't want her to think I'm hiding anything."

Suddenly, I felt French.

After Eugene got out of the taxi, I asked Corby what he thought. "Honestly?" he said.

"Of course not," I said.

Corby was quiet for a while. Then he said, "I liked his reading glasses." Corby started to hop up the steps, using a knobby stick he'd found in the park as a cane. He stopped to catch his breath.

"Why don't you use the banister and I'll hold your stick?" I said.

Corby hopped upward. "I happen to like this stick," he said.

He stopped hopping long enough to say, "I figure I'll get a pair of those glasses of his when I get old." Corby geared up to do some more hopping. "If they're still making them."

"The stick looks stupid," I said.

Corby brandished the stick. Bounding down the stairs came our next-door neighbor. Corby and his brandishing were in her way. She stopped. He stopped.

"You're not allowed to have sticks on the stairwell," she said.

"It's not a stick," he said. "It's a cane."

"I'm on the co-op board," our next-door neighbor said, trying to get past Corby. "It's a safety issue."

Corby, even with his walking cast, was able to parry her every move. "Did you know that every year more than one hundred people visit emergency rooms because of cane accidents?" he said. "And that forty-two percent of people in this country do not know what forty-two percent means?"

While Corby was making up these statistics, our next-door neighbor snuck past him.

A few days later, the president of the board called to talk to Corby, but by then he had moved out. The hopping had started to take its toll. He was living in an elevator building with an old friend, Bebe Ottie, who'd gotten in touch with Corby after she discovered that her boyfriend was not the man he said he was:

Alvaro Espinoza, the shortstop for the Yankees. Bebe began to get suspicious when he didn't go to spring training, supposedly because of an injury. It turned out he couldn't even throw a ball. He had the drug problem, though. Bebe was in a state. And she had a spare room.

Around the same time Corby moved in with Bebe Ottie, Eugene called to tell me that his analyst had had a stroke that left him unable to speak.

Freudian analyst . . . can't speak . . . where's the problem? I thought, but Eugene sounded troubled by the news so I said, "Was he sick?"

"Not even faintly," Eugene said. "It's unfathomable. I saw him just last week."

"Life is so weird," I said. Existentially profound I was not.

I heard Eugene sigh. "To let someone down that way," he said.

"I know what you mean," I said. I wasn't sure what he meant, but I took a stab. "Think of all those nutcases left high and dry."

"That's not what I mean," Eugene said. "It's that . . . for him to have a stroke like that, it's unconscionable."

"Do you mean that on account of transference, he symbolized so many different personas—fathers, mothers, brothers, sisters—to so many different people?" I said.

"No, no, that's not what I mean," Eugene said. "That's not it at all."

"Do you mean—?" but I couldn't finish the sentence because I had run out of meanings. I wished he would just tell me what he meant. "Is that your doorbell?" I said, referring to the dissonant sound on the phone.

"Perseus is playing a Chopin nocturne. Intoxicating, isn't it?" Eugene said.

"It's nice," I said. "So do you think your analyst will have to retire?"

"Yes, exactly!" Eugene said with excitement. "That's what I was trying to say!" Finally, I'd gotten the answer right. And yet, I still didn't know what Eugene meant. "It's not ethical to terminate this way. How dare he deprive me of my psychological pretext?" Then he yelled, "Perseus, keep it down in there!"

"But don't worry, darling," he said. "I'll figure something out so we can continue our mornings." Now I understood. Eugene hadn't been talking about professional ethics or protocol or therapy. He had meant that he was out of an alibi.

Weeks and weeks went by. I guess Eugene never figured out a way to continue our mornings. My parents came to town to see some shows on Broadway and to see me on my couch. I'd been sitting there for quite a while, eating fruit but not throwing it and trying to work out what it was I saw in Eugene.

"Do you have a will?" my father said after I told him about Corby's Lisfranc fracture.

"Why would I have a will?" I said.

"Adults have wills," my father said. "You never know."

"Leave her alone," my mother said. "She doesn't have anything to give away."

"Look what happened to your friend Corby," my father said.

"He's not dead," I said. "He just doesn't live here anymore."

Later that night on the way to dinner, my father said again, "I think you should get a will." I was beginning to think that either he knew something I didn't or that he was planning to murder me.

"This is not the time or the place for a discussion about wills," my mother said. We were on the bus.

"If I wanted to start a *crêperie,* would you invest in it?" I said to my father.

"You want to start a *crêperie?*" my mother said.

"No," I said.

TEN

The hen a lot of things happened. Most of them are not worth going into. The rest I'll catch you up on. Here's hoping you find even those things worth going into.

Eugene, Margaret, and Perseus moved to New Jersey. Once a month, though, Eugene saw patients late so he spent the night in the city. He stayed with me. Corby was there, too, but tended to be in the living room, teaching himself tae kwon do. Nobody should be around all that kicking and there were other reasons, too, that Eugene and I kept mostly to my room.

Corby was there, by the way, because not long after he had moved out of the apartment, he'd limped back in. Bebe Ottie, guess what, had never dated Alvaro Espinoza or an Alvaro Espinoza imposter or anyone the least bit baseball-related. This she admitted to Corby when he confronted her after finding out that her then boyfriend, supposedly the sous-chef at the governor's mansion, also did not exist. Enough about her.

Well, one more thing. Years later, I heard that she had bragged to people that Corby was one of the inventors of four-wheel drive. There is probably a name for the type of insanity she has. You know who could tell us? Eugene. He knows a lot about this area.

Too bad I can't just call him and ask, isn't it? Oh, no. Now I've done it! Gone and ruined this book. Please pretend I didn't just give away the ending. Were you thinking that Eugene and I were perfect together?

One more thing and then you're all caught up. I was working as an assistant to a celebrity whose name I had better not divulge if that's okay with you, but I can tell you she's fat and she's a lesbian and that that is not as narrow a field as you might think. My job was to buy up supplies of Dr. Nougat candy bars once a week from various stores; eat a bar from each batch; then write up reports about the taste, freshness, crispness, discoloration, if any, and whether the bars were chipped or nicked. My boss wanted only the best. It wasn't a hard job—a limo took me to each place. But you know how Karl Marx said labor can be alienating? I couldn't agree with him more.

So, let's see. Where was I? Okay. Eugene.

He used to show up in the evening after his last patient. Eugene and I had come up with a kind of routine, which began by talking about that last patient. He never told me her name because it would be unethical, but I was told everything else, including her initials and the name of the Art Deco building she lived in. And once, not entirely covering the caption with his thumb, he showed me her picture in a magazine. Our routine ended with us fooling around and talking some more about his patients' problems until we went to sleep.

I love it when someone breaks the rules, but this was even

better! Eugene was breaching professional code, merely for my amusement. It made me feel like one of the select.

You know, I really do miss hearing about those patients of Eugene's. My favorite patient, I think, was the man who said first thing to Eugene when they met, "I'm a terrible person and I feel extremely guilty about it. Please, Doctor, can you help me? I don't want to feel guilty anymore."

"Another success story," he said to me the morning we heard on the television news that the newly happy-go-lucky terrible person had been convicted for obstruction of justice and defrauding investors of thirty million dollars. Eugene wasn't technically a doctor, but that didn't stop him from doing his job. The terrible person had proceeded from guilt complex to guilty sentence. Eugene watched the rest of the news and I watched Eugene put his sweater on inside out. I didn't say anything, however, because he was running late, one; and two, what doesn't Eugene know?

Incidentally, it was the happy-go-lucky terrible-person patient of Eugene's who'd inspired me to formulate my esteem-lowering therapy aimed at anyone too big for his britches.

Listen, I'm sorry for not sticking to the story. From now on, I promise, I will tell you about Eugene with digressions called for only by common sense. But first, I have to ask: Do you think I've declined since my school days in England? That I haven't fulfilled my promise? Remember all those smart things I used to say? Or did I? Maybe I never reached a height high enough to fall from. Anyway, I hope you are not getting fed up with me because, as it happens, I think I'm beginning to like you more and more. You're a good listener. Plus, I bet you have a winning way of turning the page.

★　　★　　★

Now, really now: Eugene.

He pretty much always left my place early, usually before I had even gotten out of bed. I didn't have to start buying Dr. Nougat bars for some time after that. Life was really going my way for once.

"I hate to tell you," Corby said one day after Eugene left, "but he sneaks into the kitchen to call his wife and say good night." Corby had shaving gook all over his face. He'd walked out of the bathroom in the middle of shaving to tell me his news. That's how much he couldn't wait to make me feel bad.

"You don't know anything," I said.

"True but irrelevant," Corby said. "I don't miss anything that goes on around here. And at eleven, always at eleven on the dot, I can hear Eugene tell his wife 'I love you.'"

"He tells me the same a few hours later," I said. Corby went back to the bathroom to finish dolling himself up before physical therapy. For this was the day Corby was planning to tell his therapist he was in love with her.

"Does anyone really say 'I love you' unless they're in the movies or they're trying to get something out of the other person?" I said. Corby was ironing his gym shorts on the kitchen counter. I was turning the pages of *The New York Times* as if I cared about the world.

Every once in a while, for effect, I said, "Hmmph," or "How do you like that!" or "What do you know?"

Corby never did tell his therapist he loved her. But he did tell her he loved her posture. Later that day, I got fired. The celebrity accused me of telling *Candy Bar Magazine* about her Dr. Nougat habit. To my knowledge, there was never any mention in *Candy Bar Magazine* about her or about Dr. Nougats.

Besides, who else could I tell except you? And Corby. I told him. And I guess I told my mother, who told my father. I must have told my grandmother. My grandmother said I could sue and she knew a lawyer.

"Everyone knows a lawyer," my father said to my grandmother.

I also told a few other people you don't know and I hardly do, either. You don't know someone named Sonny, do you? I told him. The point is: Never tell anyone anything you don't want spread around. What I really mean is don't tell me.

"I'm sorry to see you go," the celebrity said to me, "because you have a delicate palate." See me go? She fired me. This gave me a lot of time to get ready for my next Monthly Eugene Visit. I was supposed to be looking for a job.

I spent a lot of time at the gym. One day, while I was on the rowing machine, a guy who was cute seemed to be eyeing me. I saw him write something on a scrap of paper, which he then laid on the floor near the rowing machine. There was a sense of urgency about him. You might even say lewdness. Wow, what if things worked out between this guy, who was cute, and me? And Eugene found out? And was really jealous? And then realized he'd been taking me for granted? And, and, and . . . I was pretty sure the guy who was cute couldn't take his eyes off me now— his stare was that fierce. I was dying to take a peek at the note he'd written, but I played it blasé and finished my full routine and then some, to impress him. Only then did I pick up the scrap of paper. I tried not to sweat. The note said "Asshole, you're not allowed on the equipment more than twenty minutes!!!"

Also: One night at a party I met a guy who worked in the PR department at the National Kidney Foundation. "We're the number-eight killer!" he said, the same way a guy would tell you his team made the play-offs.

So much for no more digressions. Except here is a disquieting thought: What if all the years I spent with Eugene were in the end merely one long digression?

I guess everything is.

Eugene reentered the picture a week ahead of schedule. He was to give a paper to a group called Psychiatrists Without Borders and invited me. The thesis of Eugene's lecture was that Thanatos, the wish to die, is stronger than Eros, the wish to live. In making his case, Eugene had used phrases from two dead languages and also a dialect spoken by the Sioux Indians. The breadth of Eugene's arcana bowls me over even today. At the dinner afterward, Margaret and I sat next to each other. Eugene had devised the seating plan. You could read a lot into that. The first thing I'd like to suggest reading is that it illustrates Eugene's thesis.

"You don't look a hundred percent," I said to Margaret. "Are you okay?" In retrospect, I appreciate how this was not the right thing to say, even with that ultra-caring voice of mine. I guess I thought Margaret would be pleased. I guess I thought she liked to play the sick card as a way of getting sympathy, much as I do, from time to time. I guess I thought nobody likes to hear the contrary—"you look healthy"—because isn't that just another way of saying you're fat? That's what I thought consciously; what I thought subconsciously, only others can say. But I agree with you.

The other reason I had made the remark was that after ten minutes on the topic, I'd run out of things to say on whether or not the salad dressing had been made with anchovies.

"Excuse me?" Margaret said. She didn't mean that she hadn't heard what I'd said or that she had accidentally kicked me.

"Haven't you been unwell?" I said. Margaret folded her program and she folded it again, then again. "You have asthma," I said. "That's why you moved to New Jersey. The air is better." They say it is mathematically impossible to fold a piece of paper in half more than eight times. They say this, but I think Margaret might have proved them wrong. "For your asthma," I said. I don't know if this had cleared up matters for Margaret, but for me, questions had been raised. For instance, did they even live in New Jersey?

I didn't want to get Eugene in trouble, though. "You know what?" I said. "I was thinking of someone else. You look healthy." I couldn't tell you what Margaret was thinking. She said something like thank you. "Darn healthy," I said. Let her think I thought she was fat, I didn't care.

From then on, it was never the same with Margaret and me. But I quickly forgave Eugene. My magnanimity, as we've seen over and over, can be bountiful. Margaret, meanwhile, turned to the man sitting on her other side, presumably a psychiatrist without a border, and chatted gaily until she got up, pronounced the word "babysitter," and left.

The group retired to the lobby for coffee and Fig Newtons. After I'd had my fill, I waved good-bye to Eugene, who seemed to be listening with rigor to a woman wearing a cardigan buttoned all wrong. The woman jabbed the air in front of Eugene's face with her Fig Newton, presumably to emphasize her point, which I later learned from Eugene was that it was high time for a new version of the play *Oedipus,* but told from the point of view of the Sphinx. Eugene held up a finger to signal that I should wait and it got whacked by the woman's cookie. Not too long after that, Eugene's arm was locked with mine and he was steering me out the front door. Margaret was . . . I don't know where Margaret was.

The instant our feet hit the sidewalk, Eugene gave me an exuberant hug. Lest you be too happy for me, you should know that Eugene soon disappeared to make a telephone call.

While Eugene was in the phone booth, I waited on the curb, trying to strike the pose of someone who had important things to do. Taxicab drivers must have surmised I had places to go. They stopped. I sent them away. Eventually Eugene returned. He looked a little blue, or maybe the sun was in his eyes. "Might you not come to Detroit with me tomorrow?" he said.

"Detroit?" I said. "I have never been to Detroit. They say it is . . ." I couldn't think of a single good way to end that sentence. Can you? For instance, "the Paris of the Midwest" doesn't work. "I hear it is the motor capital," was what I said. And then, "Yes, I would love to go."

Eugene was to be the keynote speaker at a conference on dreams. "You're just saying that to get me into bed," I said. Eugene nodded. Had he not heard me? Or had he simply not been as charmed by my sally as I, for instance, was? Eugene told me he would have invited me earlier but Margaret had been planning to join him. At the last minute she decided against it on account of her asthma. He said.

"Poor Margaret," I said—and no matter who was telling the truth, she *was* poor Margaret.

The Psychiatrists Without Borders were starting to seep out of the building. One, who still had his plastic cup of coffee, tapped Eugene on the shoulder. The man wanted to know whether Eugene thought there was anything below the subconscious.

"You're querying what's down there underneath the subconscious?" Eugene said in a tone that implied the answer. This is a nice trick if one can manage to pull it off.

"I see," said the man in a tone that implied he did not.

"Excuse me," I said. "I have an engagement." I did and I didn't. There was a department store down the street that was still open.

This is what I packed for the overnight to Detroit: one pair houndstooth Capris; two off-the-shoulder sweatshirts (different shoulders); three bathing suits and something to wear over them, though I'd have rather been dead than go swimming in public; shoes, shoes, shoes; many socks and then some more socks; something to sleep in that was provocative and another thing to sleep in that would make anyone turn over and go to sleep; that drab long skirt I had brought to England (in case I met the Queen); my grandmother's old pearls (possibly real); one damaged straw pocketbook at a bargain price; one make-up palette; two identical "one-of-a-kind" combination traveling hair dryer and alarm clocks; some novels so it didn't look as though I was just a companion (which, of course, I was); hair accessories; art supplies (I've always wanted to learn to sketch); one box of chocolates for Eugene; and a shoehorn.

My aunt Sugar called that night, just as I was pondering whether Eugene would fancy me more in cap sleeves or dolman sleeves. Aunt Sugar's women's consciousness–raising group was to be in New York the next day, celebrating their twenty-year reunion by going to a Broadway show and getting their hairs dyed by the top colorists at the top salons. In between, she wanted to take me to dinner. I, as you know, would be in Detroit with Eugene, but I sure wasn't going to tell Aunt Sugar, who would blab it to my mother, who would get her hopes up. "You don't have a job any longer, is that what I heard?" Aunt Sugar said.

"As a matter of fact," I said, "I will be flying to Cleveland tomorrow for a major television interview." Detroit sounded too improbable, and Los Angeles, the logical place, too blatant.

I threw both tops into my suitcase and, for good measure, one with tulip sleeves. You probably already know this about me, but I overpack for everything—once even jury duty.

"Cleveland?" Aunt Sugar said. "There are no shows produced in Cleveland. Are you sure you don't mean Pittsburgh?"

"Yes," I said, "I'm flying to Cleveland, but the job must be in Pittsburgh." Then I managed to tell Aunt Sugar good-bye. There was my shirt with leg-of-mutton sleeves to consider, but remember: this was Detroit we are talking about.

One-Mississippi, two-Mississippi, three-Mississippi seconds later, the phone rang. "A job in Cincinnati!" my mother said. "That's exciting! We know the best place to eat there. I'll look it up. I think I know where I put the file."

It occurred to me that I had to wash my hairbrush. "Mom," I said, "I'm in the middle of something."

"Aunt Sugar will know the name," my mother said. "Should I call her now?"

"The one thing I don't need are the names of places to eat in Cincinnati," I said.

"You don't have to eat any candy bars for this job, do you?" my mother said.

When my mother found out I didn't have a job in Cincinnati, she put my father on the line. "What happened to the job in Cincinnati?" my father said. "It sounded nifty."

"It's Cleveland," I said.

"Cleveland," my father said. "Much better, although I'm told they have a museum in Cincinnati that isn't bad for a second-rate city. Or am I thinking even Indianapolis?"

Corby came in and flopped onto the bed. So much for stacks of clothes. Evidently, folding meant zip to Corby. Tissue paper even less. "That thing is on TV again," he said. Corby started to go through my stuff.

I covered the mouthpiece of the phone. "Get out of here," I said. Corby didn't budge.

While Corby is rummaging through my stuff and my father opining about the cultural institutions of St. Joe, Missouri, don't you think now might be a good time for a little gossip? It's about you. No, of course, the gossip isn't about you, you silly goose. It turns out a friend of mine had run into my aunt Sugar in a coffee shop on Second Avenue. He knew her from Parents Weekend at Camp Rodeph Tomahawk, if that was the name. Aunt Sugar's son had been in my friend's bunk. Anyway, Aunt Sugar was with a man she said was from the UN. It was eight thirty. Broadway shows started at eight. You see what I'm saying? Don't tell Uncle Walt.

On second thought, you can tell Uncle Walt anything you please about Aunt Sugar as long as you don't say you got it from me.

With all the time that went by, you'd think I'd be off the phone. Wrong. My father was giving me advice about retirement accounts.

"It's just an interview, Daddy," I said. "I'm flying there tomorrow, so forget I even mentioned it."

"Who's paying for this trip?" my father said.

"They are," I said, "and it's first-class." No matter what happened, I knew that would make my father happy.

"I'm in the middle of packing right now," I said truthfully. As you know, it had been a long time since I had spoken the truth. "I'll call you later, it's a promise."

Can you believe I almost missed my flight? In the taxi, halfway to the airport, it struck me: I hadn't packed my beige espadrilles. Maybe you could go to Detroit without your beige espadrilles, but I don't have that kind of pluck. By the time my beige espadrilles and I finally got to Gate B32, the plane was boarding and Eugene was nowhere in sight. I took my seat. What else could I do? Part of me was beginning to believe I really did have an important job interview in Detroit. A man assigned to a row near the bathroom asked if the seat next to me was empty. Of course it was, but I said it was taken.

We would have taken off without Eugene, I think, but there was a holdup because the troop of Boy Scouts in the back of the plane wouldn't sit down. I was grateful to the Scouts, even though I considered their presence on the plane a bad omen. (It is a pet theory of mine that a flight that counts among its passengers any group of children—a hockey team, a marching band, kids on their way to summer camp, for example—is more likely to crash because of the page-one newspaper potential.)

The Scouts sat down and I tried to look as if I were paying attention to the emergency evacuation lesson or whatever it's called, not because I thought it would be of use, but because you know me: polite.

In the nick of time, Eugene ran down the aisle, out of breath. He didn't look so hot.

Eugene didn't bother to stow his carry-on in the overhead bin. He collapsed into his seat and tilted it back to the limit. He sighed. "I almost missed the plane, too," I said—a show of support, I hoped. I poised myself to tell the story of the beige espadrilles, but it didn't come up.

The plane took off. "I have news," Eugene said. He put his hand on mine. Then he turned his head away. "Astonishing, dismal news," the profile of Eugene said.

A flight attendant walked briskly over to tell him that his seat had to be in an upright position. Eugene didn't seem to hear. His news, I was sure, was too astonishing and dismal for that. In fact, it was so astonishing and dismal that before he could tell me, he had to fortify himself with some alcohol on the rocks. Then he said, "Are you sitting down?" He could see that I was, so I didn't say anything. I was trying to be sophisticated. I nodded. "It appears that my marriage may be on the brink of disassembly," Eugene said.

We sat in silence, he thinking I know not what and I thinking that his news was hunky-dory. I believe I managed to look as rattled as Eugene.

"I always did wonder about you and Margaret," I said.

"Is that so?" Eugene said. "Did you not suppose us befitting and content?"

"I had my doubts," I said.

"Hmmm," Eugene said, sounding stumped. Eugene, as you've heard, is brainy, but what I'd said seemed beyond his grasp.

I don't mind telling you that the trip did not live up to my expectations. Eugene was not himself. Or maybe he was and that was the problem. "Failure is not part of my heritage," he said on the way up to our room, which was lovely, by the way. "My grandfather was a contender for the Nobel Prize in Economics."

After the guy who had carried our luggage left, Eugene stood at the window. We had a partial view of the pool. "How could this happen to me?" he said, all forlorn. "Did you know that my parents have had the same housekeeper for more than thirty years?"

"That's nice," I said.

"And how about us?" Eugene said, making his case with vigor. "Look how long we've known each other."

Really, I don't mean this to sound snobby or elitist, but for Eugene to compare my tenure with the housekeeper's wasn't the most flattering thing anyone's ever said to me.

I started to unpack, but not everything because that kind of excess, I felt, would look stupid in light of the mood.

Eugene singled out one of the swimmers and asked me if I thought she looked like Simone de Beauvoir. That's the kind of question you worry is a trick question.

"A little," I said.

Eugene disappeared into the bathroom, where for the longest time, he was either on the phone or talking to himself. He was holed up so long that he almost missed his lecture. At last, he reappeared, kissed me good-bye on the forehead, and said he was sorry but no guests allowed at the conference. On his way out the door, he turned on the television. "For old times, perhaps you should turn on the telly and watch Wimbledon," he said.

Things did get a little better. In bed that night, Eugene looked into my eyes. "I so longed for you to have been in the audience," he said. "You would have been amused." Eugene stretched his leg so it crossed over mine.

At LaGuardia Airport the next day, before we went our separate ways, Eugene said, "You will always be a part of my life, my forever you." He gave me a big kiss. "I count on that."

A few days after I got back from Detroit, my grandmother died. It was sad. My father gave a eulogy in which he included the detail that my grandmother, his mother, had been helpful to me with my Belarus sketch. By dying, my grandmother had helped out again because nobody asked me anything about Detroit.

After the service, my mother said, "I have an idea. Why don't you write your eulogy for me now, so I can help you with it?" As a matter of fact, this was not such a bad idea. Try this: The next time your mother dies and you must give the eulogy, look up from your notes, and say, "Mother helped me with that line," or "This part coming up is the part that Mother liked a lot."

"That is pure Jessica Mitford," I said to my mother about her idea, "combined with pure Evelyn Waugh." I hadn't studied in England for nothing.

"You know, Grandma was so proud of you," my mother said. "But she did want you to finish your thesis." I have to say that that remark made me less raring to go with the old eulogy.

"So now I'm off the hook!" I said. What I could also have pointed out, but even I had obnoxiousability limits, was that I wasn't the only quitter in the family. My sister had just left her husband of ten years. Just kidding. I don't have a sister. I swear I would have told you if I had.

My parents had, in truth, just quit their book club. Rather, the club had been disbanded because none of the members could get through *Absalom, Absalom!* "Do you *get* fiction?" my father had said to me when he was on page 163, the last page of that book he read. It is a curious fact—isn't it?—that *Absalom, Absalom!* had also brought down Corby's parents' book club and one other book club I heard about. If I had been smart, I would have written my thesis about the *Absalom, Absalom!* phenomenon instead of whatever topic it was I had chosen. (Bet you can't remember.)

ELEVEN

This is what Eugene said when I called him from Philadelphia. "I have someone in my office now, dear, but I will call anon because I need to talk to you." Then he paused psychoanalytically.

"You do?" I said.

"Not *need*," he said. "Did I say I need to talk to you? Long. I am *longing* to talk to you." No pause. Eugene hung up.

That was the conversation verbatim. No "good-bye," nothing. I know because immediately after it happened, I wrote the whole thing down so I could ask everyone for an exegesis. Here is what some of them had to say:

Lisa: "Something's going on and it's not good."

Deb: "He's back together with Margaret. No question about it."

Meg: "No wonder that woman is divorcing him."

Joan: "He talks like a character in a remaindered novel."

Pearson: "I hate it when anyone refers to 'my office.' Seems so show-offy."

Susan: "It's uncanny. That is almost identical to what Robert told me right before we broke up."

Phil: "You should have told him you'd stay on the line until he was free to talk. Someone did that to me once and I was so unnerved, I broke up with her on the spot."

Buffy: "He's either having an affair or a breakdown, but most likely, both."

Cynthia: "He's a shrink so I assume when he says he needs you, he's subconsciously saying he kneads you, like bread. But what's *that* supposed to mean? That he molds you into shape, maybe? Except, of course, then he says he doesn't knead you."

Larry: "How do I know what he means? I'm a guy."

Mark: "It's a guy thing."

Jeff: "What kind of guy would say a thing like that?"

Martha: "Can't tell you what it means, but I can tell you what it does not mean: that he has any intention of calling you again."

Sarah: "He treats you worse than dirt. What's worse than dirt?"

Phoebe: "As you know, I have always thought he was a piece of shit."

Lady sitting next to me on the bus: "Can I be blunt, honey? I don't think he likes you."

Nina: "I'd be more than happy to spy on him. You want me to? I could call in sick and do it tomorrow."

Esther: "Do you think Eugene knows anyone who could get me tickets to *Midsummer Night's Dream*?"

Ann: "Remind me who Eugene is again."

Corby: *"Anon?"*

★   ★   ★

As usual, I was the only one who had a kind word on the topic of Eugene, the only one with a happy take on what he had to say. And yes: Eugene didn't call back. And yes: everyone was correct that despite Eugene's "longing," the total time he had not talked to me when I'd called was about twenty-three seconds. But no one had taken into consideration that someone had been in his office and it's not easy to open your heart under the shadow of a third party. Or, as in my case, numerous parties.

"The phone's free!" a million people said as soon as I opened my parents' bedroom door, after talking to Eugene and then some of my confidantes. Had there been a heart attack in the house? Had the bathroom pipes burst? Fire in the kitchen? No. We were out of ice. It had to be dealt with. An ice person had to be called.

"And whom were you talking to in there for so long?" Aunt Sugar said. "A beau?" Two million ears listened in.

There were so many things I could have said to Aunt Sugar to shut her up—things along the lines of, say, how did she like the play that she didn't go to because she was having dinner at a coffee shop with a man who was not from the UN and was not Uncle Walt.

"It was about the job in Detroit," I said, knowing no good would come of it.

But that's typical of me. "This is going to end in tears," I tell myself every time I balance a cup of coffee on the upholstered arm of the chair I'm sitting on. And then, lo and behold, the cup topples and even before it lands, I tell myself, "Told me so!" Not to spell out, or spill out, one of the metaphors of my life, but I always do the stupid thing and then I do it again. I never learn.

"Detroit?" Aunt Sugar said. "What happened to the job in

Pittsburgh? You said you were flying to Cleveland for a job in Pittsburgh."

"The producer decided to move the show," I said. "He thought there was too much coal in Pittsburgh."

Lucky for me: Someone said, "Sugar, who delivers the best ice?" And Sugar, with a job to do, was off.

The next day, so was I—supposedly to Detroit for my follow-up interview, but really to New York, I hoped, to reunite with Eugene, whom, I hoped, was equally eager to reunite with me. Or at least willing.

A man answered Eugene's phone at his office and said Eugene was away on vacation. I unpacked and called back again. Maybe the man had been mistaken. Maybe I had coincidentally called the number of a different Eugene, the vacation-going Eugene. Maybe "vacation" was what the fellows at the Emmerlich Psychoanalytic Institute called the bathroom. Maybe Margaret had . . . anything is possible when you make up your mind; only it didn't turn out to be possible.

Eugene returned a couple weeks later, or at least that's the point at which he answered his phone. He looked to be in high spirits as he walked through my door. He was tan and trimmer than I'd ever seen him. "What a gloomy time it is but for you, my lambency," he said.

"I was in Philadelphia, but I've been back for a while," I said because I was only 65 percent sure what "lambency" meant.

"Do tell," Eugene said, and I was about to but instead he told me that he had taken Perseus to a resort on Long Island to cheer him up and also there was a sublime golf course there.

"It was so important to spend time with Perseus at this juncture," Eugene said. He told me that Perseus had been on a soccer team at the resort and that one day he filled in for the referee. "I can't tell you how good it felt to run up and down that field with my new body," he said. "Did you notice I've lost thirteen pounds since my sadness?" I saw Eugene caress his midriff, which was now minus the pudge.

The only fan in my apartment was in the kitchen, so we pulled up stools and sat in front of it. I recommend doing this if you like riding in a convertible. I do not.

"It was my heart's desire to call you the whole time," Eugene said, "but can you believe, there are no telephones in all of Montauk, my special seraph?" Can you? The fan blew a piece of dust or something in my eye.

I was about to tell Eugene that my grandmother had died, but he said, "I think I'll get through this." He placed his hand on my fan-blown hair and calmly said, "Rest assured."

Then he headed toward the refrigerator. "Do you have any water?" he said. "I must confess to having a soupçon of a hangover." If Eugene had indeed returned to New York earlier that day, as he had told me, then that would have made him smashed the night before, perhaps even during his pains to make his poor, poor son feel better about the situation at home.

You can't win when someone opens your refrigerator door. Some things are better left closed, and don't forget I had Corby's foodstuff to worry about, too. What could be amiss? Plenty. Let's see. Arrangement of cold cuts too aligned; condiments sloppy; wrong amount of fruit; inferior brand of beer; cheese not foreign enough; generic mayonnaise; baloney sandwich on Wonder Bread minus two bites; fat-free pudding in a baggie; hard-boiled egg whites; stack of stale pancakes on a plate; prune juice; unwrapped lollipop touching unwrapped lettuce; stolen pats of butter; empty bottle of soy sauce; can of chocolate syrup with random receipt sticking to label; tin foil wads in an assortment of chewed-up chewing gum shapes; dog treats (no dog in the house); panty hose; one Tupperware top; mold on whatever that is; old clam dip (P-U!)

"You know where they have good water?" I said as I closed the refrigerator door heftily. "And that restaurant reviewer, what's-her-name, gave it three stars." I pulled Eugene away from the refrigerator, turned off the fan, and we went to that place.

Eugene ordered a fancy bottle of water and a fancy bottle of wine and had me believe that he had never loved Margaret. The reason he'd married her, he said, was that it had been the right thing to do. Okay, correct me if I'm wrong: Hadn't Eugene been over the moon about Margaret when they met? Besides, if Eugene hadn't been in love, wouldn't marrying Margaret have been the exactly wrong thing to do? But he was the logician and I was the irrationally infatuated one and he had lightly touched my cheek and told me that Margaret's soul did not compare with mine. So when Eugene said he had never loved Margaret, I said, "I know." Then I made a face that I hoped came across as one of sympathy, not drowsiness.

Eugene ordered another bottle of wine and explained that though he'd never loved Margaret, he deeply admired her for giving up her career so that he could move to New York to switch his career. What had been her career? "She hadn't yet settled on one, thus making her sacrifice all the more noble," Eugene said. "Perhaps she could have cured cancer someday." Perhaps Margaret could have gotten cancer someday, but given that she had no science background, it was unlikely she was ever going to cure that disease or any disease.

"Tragic," I said.

Eugene also told me that the divorce was going to be amicable, I guess because of all that admiration of his. As far as I can tell, "amicable" is a word used only to apply to divorce, especially ones that turn out to be not amicable.

While Eugene swallowed an antidepressant, I picked up the check. Eugene had only recently started taking the pills. "Do they make you feel any different?" I said as we walked home. Ever since Eugene had told me he was on something, I thought I'd sensed a change in him. Look at the devil-may-care way he reacted when the waitress informed us they had sold the last toasted coconut crepe cup with pineapple à la mode, for instance. But let's never ignore my imagination. In fact, the Eugene we were dealing with could have been the same old Eugene. (Is there, I wonder, such a thing as a secondhand placebo effect?)

"It is most extraordinary," Eugene said. "The medicine seems to have helped my golf swing. Other than that—though it hardly seems possible—I believe it has made me even more humane."

It was impossible to know if he was being facetious, so I smiled gently. We reached the corner of Broadway and something, and Eugene let go of my hand and charged across the street on a yellow light. I followed, and almost got hit by a bus.

After I survived, we turned down a side street where a homeless woman was delivering a lecture to no one I could see about how to roast a chicken the French way. As we passed, she held out a paper cup. "Rinse the *poulet* or bird and pat dry with paper towels," she said. "Don't truss—it will only add to your problems—but do use a rack."

I made a motion for my wallet and Eugene put his hand on mine to stop me. "Allow me," he said. I could not see how much money Eugene the Humane put in the hat, but it clinked.

"For a dollar," she said to us as we walked away, "I could teach you how to make the perfect gravy."

How, I couldn't tell you, but somehow this reminded Eugene that he had to get to the train station immediately. Eugene said he'd promised Margaret—he was still living with her—that he'd be back in time to drive the babysitter home. Schmaltzy good-bye, promise to call, hop in taxi, etc.

There was a note on the kitchen table when I got back. "Your father called to say call when you get back from Detroit," Corby had written. "Told him you're not in Detroit & he said you are in Detroit. So I said you aren't in Detroit and he was so put out, told him you're in Minneapolis. So whatever you do, don't call your father . . . till you 'get back' from Minneapolis! C."

Great: a brand-new city I had to learn about before I could talk to my parents.

The phone rang and rang again. It rang all night; and I let it ring. It could have been my father putting two and two together. Early the next morning, Eugene showed up. He hugged me with the fervor of someone who's spent the past week lost on a mountaintop and has just been rescued by the forest ranger. When he got over that, he stepped back and noticed my T-shirt. "Poetically apt," he said.

"Sorry," I said. "I didn't have time to change." What I was wearing was what I'd slept in and it wasn't something you want anyone to know about. Oh, but you can know: a Helen Keller T-shirt. Someone had given me the shirt and it was soft is all I can offer in defense.

"You didn't run into Helen Keller, did you?" Of course that didn't make sense, but neither did anything else.

"The opposite," Eugene said. "I have been blind and deaf to Margaret."

I tensed up. "Oh, my God," I said, covering up Helen Keller's nose, one of the few things that had worked for her. "Is the divorce . . . off?"

"Alas, baby doll, I fear Margaret has crossed the Rubicon," Eugene said, "and what choice have I but to follow." What he meant, as he explained later in the comfort of my bedroom, was that he had discovered the night before that Margaret was having an affair. However happy Margaret might be over that development, trust me, I was happier.

"Now I know how Charles Bovary felt," Eugene said. "And to add insult to injury, her fellow doesn't even have tenure." We must give Eugene credit for not allowing irony to persuade him; for remember, I had not even finished writing my PhD dissertation.

Eugene brushed a strand of hair off my face and said, "Your features are lovely in this shadow." We talked about betrayal (what saddened him most was that he could no longer trust the mother of his child) and Perseus (though he wished it could be otherwise, he recognized that his son would despise him for the next five years) and living alone (aside from missing the way the morning light used to stream into his bedroom window, he seemed rather jolly about his new setup) and his work (he believed that the later work of the French psychoanalyst Jacques Lacan was derivative of Eugene's early work, which was an audacious theory, in my opinion, since Eugene hadn't entered Lacan's field of work until Lacan was dead) and family (nothing could be more meaningful, according to Eugene) and love (nothing could be more meaningful, according to Eugene) and self-determination (nothing could be more meaningful, according to Eugene).

Once again, I feel it behooves me to explain to you why I remained so fixed on Eugene even though he was someone I would normally have made fun of and certainly satirize in, say, a book. Maybe it was because he was . . . no. Maybe it was because I was . . . no. Maybe it could be chalked up to all those years that . . . no. Maybe it was the way he . . . no. Maybe it was his big . . . no. Maybe his little . . . no. Maybe he represented . . . no. Maybe I didn't really want someone who . . .

no. Maybe there was nobody else that . . . no. In lieu of explanation, will you accept acknowledgment?

"Wouldn't it be grand if I could lie here all day with you?" Eugene said. Then he leapt out of bed and made a beeline for his clothes, which were folded neatly on an empty bookshelf. "But unhappily for us," Eugene said, "there is a sorry old chap with generalized anxiety disorder who awaits my attention and what he thinks is my empathy from nine o'clock until . . ." Eugene looked at his watch. "Oh, my. Already late." Eugene kissed my arm twice. "While my patient is perseverating about whether he should get the air conditioner with eleven thousand BTUs or twelve thousand BTUs, I will be thinking only of you, carnally of you." Eugene walked to the door, where he stopped and turned around to smooth down his hair and to say, "Margaret is a bitch, is she not?" He waved good-bye and told me he'd call anon.

That time, I didn't fall for the anon thing. To tell you the truth, I hadn't completely fallen for it before, either. I had a feeling, deep down, maybe not from the beginning but from before the middle, for sure before year five of the ten that I'd known Eugene, that he was bullshitting me. About everything, but mostly my place in his heart. They say you know everything, but you don't really *know;* what you have is a pretty good idea. It's the uncertainty that keeps you in the game. They also say you'd be surprised how little you know about someone. I'm an optimist so I find that hopeful. By the way, I don't have any problem believing that one sort of knows everything and nothing at the same time and I hope you can live with that, too.

Let's review. No job under my belt, unless you count the fake job my parents thought I had. No marketable skills, let alone no doctorate. (Wait, I can type and I can make hors d'oeuvres.) No savings, as I had spent the last chunk of my

Taped But Proud money on membership to a health club that I never went to because it was too far away. But never mind. Margaret had a boyfriend and Eugene said he'd call me anon. Life was never better.

It took me a while to catch on that Eugene had disappeared. Not Jimmy Hoffa disappeared or milk carton disappeared. I mean I hadn't heard from him for a long time. For all I knew, others had. I left messages at Eugene's office, but he never called back.

On a day when it seemed particularly hard to be me—eleven weeks exactly since Eugene had said he'd call anon—on that day, I received a package with foreign stamps and no return address. Inside was a . . . was it a robe or a blanket or a tent? Whatever it was, it was made of bright orange and maroon silk and trimmed with braided edges. A letter inside explained. "My long-lost friend, enclosed is a *deel*—no, not exactly a poncho, but the traditional dress of Mongolia, where I am living in a *ger* that has no electricity. There are no windows in my *ger* either and thus no curtains, though if there were, I would arrange them so that they were fully drawn with a double twist on the left. . . ." Such a curtain position, according to the intricate code Libby and I had devised, signaled, "Miss you." Libby's letter went on to say that she had come to Mongolia with a guy in the import-export trade interested in buying up indigenous felt art. She was no longer with this guy, but had gotten a job teaching English. She proposed that when she returned to England, she, Obax, and I have a reunion and she also wrote that in Mongolia, it is rude to cross an area where women are milking cows.

I hope you don't think I'm a mushball when I tell you that I sort of choked up when I read the letter. I was also slightly troubled that Libby, who was so conversant with Anglo-Saxon,

Norse, and Celtic, was not making better use of her education. Sorry to sound so schoolmarmish, but that's what long-lost friends are for.

I tried on the *deel* and somehow this seemed to give me the courage to call Eugene's house in New Jersey. I know this sounds corny but it's what Libby would have done. I had never telephonically trespassed on Eugene before.

I used what I refer to as my "generic foreign accent." Margaret answered and said, in the detached and courteous way you would if someone had dialed the wrong number, that there was no Eugene there. By the way, I thought I heard the voice of a man in the background, but I can't rule out the TV.

Once you do something against your better judgment, it gets easier to do something else against your better judgment, and pretty soon, you're doing things against everyone's better judgment.

What I did after I hung up with Margaret was wait a few minutes and then call her again. I don't have another accent in my repertoire so I spoke with a lisp. This time I said I was selling men's Dopp kits and wanted to speak to the man in the house. Margaret hung up without mentioning the man. I called again, this time holding my nose, but hung up as soon as she said hello. I remembered that telephone calls could be traced if you stayed on the line for a certain number of seconds, which for some reason I think is eleven.

Nothing could stop me now—not dejection, not humiliation, not feeling pathetic, not fear of getting in trouble, and certainly not common sense. I got on a bus. Two blocks from the Emmerlich Psychoanalytic Institute, I got off the bus, not exactly muttering to myself, but whatever is one grade less crazy than that.

Has this ever happened to you? You do something against

your better judgment—for instance, go on a desperate hunt to find someone who most likely doesn't want to be found—and in the midst of the pursuit, it dawns on you, Hey, this is entirely dumb. However, by that time, you have crawled so far out on the dumb branch that turning around seems out of the question. So with the fervor of someone storming a nursery school to free the children held hostage inside, I blew into the institute. The lobby was empty except for a bunch of about five people standing around nodding their heads and smoking. As I recall, the place looked better when the Psychiatrists Without Borders were milling about with their coffee and Fig Newtons. But maybe it was the Fig Newtons.

"I need to see Eugene Obello immediately," I said to the receptionist on the third floor, who was Xeroxing memos about the new policy aimed at cutting back the number of superfluous memos. On the counter that separated her from me, there was a bowl with peppermint hard candies. There is no amount of hungry that I could ever be that would cause me to take one of those candies. If we were talking about Fig Newtons, on the other hand, or Lorna Doones or Mallomars . . . well, there's no need to make a list here of cookies I have loved. Let's leave it at this: I blamed Eugene for the bowl of candy. I was starting to blame him for a lot of things.

It's about time, isn't it? As you probably figured out pages ago, Eugene had been lying to me and deceiving me and disappointing me since the day he entered my life almost ten years before. I take it back: the "disappointing me" part I grasped from the get-go. So why, after enduring so much so long, did I come to be enlightened only at that moment? Why put my foot down now?

As a way of answering, let me ask you—and please forgive me if I've already asked; it's a question I think about a lot: What makes a person who's always wanted to take up the banjo but never gotten around to it sign up for lessons one day? Why does a person who's never managed to stay on a diet more than a week wake up one morning full of such caloric discipline that rumors of anorexia can eventually be heard? Where does a person, age seventy-seven, find the courage to write the first sentence of a first novel? How is it that you just now came to realize that what your mother said about Trudy Hornig is true? How to explain a decision to propose marriage, move to the French countryside, redo an old kitchen, quit smoking, have a child, convert to Catholicism, order the spaghetti with marinara sauce instead of your usual, go back to school, come out of the closet, try a new career, get in touch with your high school girlfriend, go blond, switch to another brand, sit over there?

In other words, why does anyone make a change when there are so many reasons not to? Is it that at some point, a crucial grain is added to the other grains? I don't know. It really may be, as I think it was in my case, about, hmm, time.

Here we are again, back at the counter on the third floor of the institute where I am not eating peppermint candy. "Dr. Obello is with a patient," the receptionist told me in a voice that was far more solicitous than the one I had heard her use a little earlier when informing a young man she couldn't possibly give him a key to the bathroom right then because she was in the middle of important Xeroxing. "Could you take a seat, hon?" she said to me. "But if it's an emergency . . ." She had left her Xerox post at the sight of me, and I had a theory why. See if you think I'm right: she'd concluded I was a patient of Eugene's about to go home and look around for a ledge.

"That's okay," I said, trying to sound sane because it was too embarrassing otherwise. "He's not an MD, you know. He's a

PhD," I said, trying to convey definite disapproval while seeming to sound matter-of-fact.

The receptionist did not say anything. I had a hunch she didn't want to risk upsetting me. She nodded in the agreeable way someone would if she had a gun to her head. She offered me a glass of water, but I declined. "I don't have time for water," I said. She took a stealthy step away from me.

Whoever was in the office with Eugene was getting his or her money's worth. Even the next patient had been waiting forever. Normally, I don't mind waiting in a waiting room. I think about all of the other ways I could be spending my time—defrosting my refrigerator, paying bills, buying a lamp. I like the fact that nobody in sight is related to me through work or blood, and that the ringing phones are not ringing for me. The magazines, the same ones I never open at home, are ever so much more entertaining in a waiting room. Waiting in a waiting room is time off from life.

But not that day. That day the waiting was making me tense. What was taking so long? I knew exactly who was in there with Eugene, thanks to those stories he had told me when he slept over. Eugene was with the Lollipop Man, called such by Eugene because he sucked on a lollipop to calm himself.

The patient who had been waiting forever asked me if I was new. I knew exactly who that patient was, too, of course. She was the bulimic. I'm pretty sure I never told you about her because the details were so disgusting. The receptionist did not offer her any water; we could speculate why.

"You're not supposed to talk to patients," I said because I really didn't feel like talking to her.

"How else can we meet anyone?" the bulimic said. "Dr. Obello says I should reach out to people." If Eugene had, in fact, said that, I thought, then he wasn't the person I thought he was.

You don't know how tempted I was to lean over and say to her, "How many bowls of cereal last night?" Instead, I made a noncommittal "huh" sound.

We waited a longer time than I had ever thought it was possible for a human being to wait. I started to wonder if this was Eugene's trick: make them wait so long, years even, that when you appear, they really appreciate you.

Finally, I gave in. I asked the bulimic if the wait was always this exasperating. From the look on her face, you'd think I'd asked her to the prom. I guess she was happy to make conversation.

She leaned in and said confidentially, "Dr. Obello always takes a long time with this one because she has a phobia about being alone. Do you know what that's called?"

She?! She?! She?! Wasn't Eugene supposed to be with the Lollipop Man?

The door to Eugene's office opened. A very pretty girl walked out. I'm no psychiatrist but I'd say she didn't look as if she had isolophobia, fear of being alone.

Part 4

THE END
OF HIM

TWELVE

After my uncle Stuey was in a fatal rope tow accident on the bunny slope of Mount Lucky, my father called me to break the news. "Just because Uncle Stuey's dead," my father said, "doesn't mean I'm going to say I liked him."

After Eugene died, a lot of what I felt was relief (that rarely mentioned stage of mourning). This is a terrible thing to say and surely it speaks to a lack of imagination on my part, but sometimes when I'm in a bad relationship, the only solution that I can come up with is for the guy to die. Uncle Stuey notwithstanding, it is in my opinion much easier to feel love, charity, and forgiveness toward a dead person than toward a living reminder of every little thing that went wrong. And it certainly helps that there is no longer anyone left back here on earth who knows firsthand what a doormat I was in the whole affair.

For me, death speeds up the healing process.

Eugene's memorial service is at the Princeton University chapel. Evidently, one of the perks of attending Princeton as an undergraduate is that after you die, your loved and/or guilty ones can pay tribute to you in an immense Gothic Revival place of worship with pews made of oak intended for Civil War gun carriages, one of those pews having been carved with the answers to Mademoiselle Handelshomme's French literature midterm in 1938. I am sitting behind that pew.

Margaret and Perseus are, as protocol dictates, in the first row. I have a partial view of Margaret but it is decent enough to allow me to keep careful track of how many times she sheds a tear. Zero, so far. From the looks of it, what Perseus has in his hand, the gizmo that seems to be capturing his full attention, is a video game or an abacus. Is the round little man who is constantly blotting his forehead with a handkerchief and sitting next to Margaret her boyfriend? I sort of hope, for her sake, he is not. Behind me, I hear a lady say, "Sarah Jane, I told you before. The reason there are no relatives is because they had the real service in St. Louis."

No matter. There must be three hundred in attendance, easy. A full house at your funeral is one of the advantages of dying young. You can count on the group being attractive, too. Judging by how much pound cake the youthful bunch seated in the back grabbed at the pre-service reception, however, I'd say a good portion of the grievers don't know who Eugene was, but are hungry. And among those who do know Eugene, I'd say—judging this time by intuition—that they knew him *exceedingly* well. My conservative guess is that Margaret and I have been ten-timed. Does the sight of those sluts send me into a rage? To be sure; but the ire seems to hasten my passage from grief to recovery.

And so, I weep, though less for Eugene than for myself. I weep because though I recognize that I am better off without him, what else do I have? I weep because I wonder how much everyone at the Princeton University chapel knows about me and Eugene and whether they are giving me dirty looks on general principle or if I'm just imagining it. And I weep because one of these days I will die, too. I weep between a wall and a man who'd been Eugene's neighbor in New Jersey. To put it mildly, the man seems to have no qualms about expressing emotion through hymn-singing. In between hymns, though, he sits stolidly, appearing to fight off the brunt of his sorrow. Or he could be bored. There have been quite a few disquisitions by people with weighty credentials on topics such as Kant versus Heidegger's views of ontology—about a semester's worth. I'm assuming that you, like Eugene's neighbor, do not want to hear about them.

I'm assuming that what you do want to hear about is what happened to poor old Eugene. Don't expect any clues in that department from the obituaries. They say only that the death was untimely, but they didn't ask me for my policy on timeliness. And while I'm being that way, I must tell you the obituaries were not very long, nor did they mention Eugene's grandfather, the supposed Nobel prize contender. At the Princeton University chapel, smart money, from what I can gather, seems to be on a heart attack, with diverticulitis a close second. But when I'd told my friends about Eugene after his death was announced, this is what they had to say:

Lisa: "One thing we know it can't be. A heart attack. He didn't have a heart."

Deb: "He died of complications due to slimebucket-itis."

Meg: "The last time you saw Eugene, did he look as sick as I do now? Be honest because I'm wondering if I should go to the doctor."

Joan: "It really doesn't matter what the cause of death was as long as he suffered."

Pearson: "Clearly, Margaret knocked him off."

Susan: "When you find out what it was, let me know because I want Robert to get it, too. Did I tell you what Robert did to me the other day?"

Phil: "I hope you wear something alluring to the funeral."

Buffy: "If there is a God, you can bet He's being shitty to Eugene right now."

Cynthia: "Let's not forget he was a shrink, so his disease, we have to assume, and Eugene would want us to assume, was some sort of message from his subconscious. That's why I'm going to say colon cancer or colon something."

Larry: "It's so fucking cool that you used to do it with someone who croaked."

Mark: "Find out if he had just had a stress test. Have you ever noticed how many guys die after their stress test?"

Jeff: "I never thought I'd say this, but now that he's dead, I feel kind of sorry for him."

Martha: "I love how this disproves the adage that only the good die young."

Sarah: "Did you know that cockroaches can live nine days without their heads?"

Phoebe: "Who cares what killed him? Can't we just be happy?"

Nina: "Did you owe him any money? Because you'll never have to pay it back."

Ann: "I'm thoroughly confused. Didn't he pop off a long time ago?"

Esther: "Do you know if Eugene donated his eyes to science? I'm volunteering for this organization and I need six more eyes by next month."

* * *

None of my friends ever understood Eugene. I'm not sure you do, either. Or maybe I haven't done a good job explaining.

But back to the Princeton University chapel, where the organist is playing a doleful rendition of Duke Ellington's "Don't Get Around Much Anymore." I can hear tee-heeing in the pews. You don't think they are tee-heeing at me, do you? (Is anyone as much a drag as the conscience-stricken?) And why do you think Eugene's receptionist just turned around so that she is facing in my direction? No matter what my friends say, I wish I could hear what Eugene would say about this stuff. He had a way with guilt.

Time for the eulogies, I guess. There is a pretty young thing on the podium—let's say we don't imagine what her connection to Eugene is. She is reading a poem by Walt Whitman or Emily Dickinson or Auden or Keats or Byron or Kahlil Gibran or one of those guys. Maybe you don't feel this way, but I think it is cheating to read a poem at a funeral. Do your homework or sit down is my motto. Anyway, the girl continues reading, slowly and deliberately in that poem-reading voice people use. Something, something, death, the winds that blow, death, death, sunlight, end o'er the road, heaven above, something, doth die, something, something, Eugene dead, but then I don't listen anymore.

Eugene dead? Dead?! No. Surely there has been a mistake. Dying is something that happens to surly teenagers driving late at night on country roads, professional football players with undetected heart problems, sailors who fail to heed radio reports about severe gale winds, little boys whose fathers keep guns in the basement, little girls who fall down wells, mountain climbers who seemed to have had experience, California families who should never have built their houses at the bot-

*tom of so much mud, country-western singers whose little planes take
off during snowstorms, Boy Scouts who will never get their merit badge
in Lightning Safety now, rappers with enemies, rock stars with bad
habits, fat comedians in hotel rooms, movie characters who cough all too
discreetly in one of the early scenes, caretaker wives whose long-suffering
spouses kicked the bucket two weeks before, women who argue with
their fervid boyfriends about who is going to get the last slice of pork
loin, darling towheaded children at birthday parties who are allergic to
the peanuts, elder statesmen you thought were already dead, hitherto
spry old ladies who fall and break a hip, seventeen-year-olds who drop
out of high school to join up and then get in the unfriendly way of
friendly fire, chain-smokers who had quit a few years ago and thought
they were out of the woods, people's grandparents, bubonic plague vic-
tims, the Kennedys.*

"If Eugene were here today, I think he would be very
pleased by the turnout," I hear another pretty girl on the
podium say. Between you and me, if Eugene were here today,
he'd probably be crying or at least pretty upset that he was dead.

*How could Eugene be dead? It's something, isn't it? He was the first
person I ever heard utter the word "frisson," the first to put his arm
around the back of my seat in a movie theater, the first I thought I
couldn't have life happiness without. He knew about my thesis tribu-
lations. And all those friends of mine from England whom I lost touch
with? Why, he knew them, too. My parents had been charmed by
Eugene when they met him so long ago at the Chinese restaurant in
Cambridge and, recently, they asked what had become of him. I told
them he moved back to Europe. You know, I think I still have some of
his towels.*

As yet another pretty girl, maybe the fifth, walks to the
podium, I hear the man in front of me whisper to a woman
next to him, "Is there a goddamn factory in the basement turning these threnodists out?"

"I'd like to read, if I may," says the pretty girl, "from a letter of recommendation Eugene wrote on my behalf when I was applying to the Yale Divinity School. But first, I want to say that he did this even though I had not known him as my professor per se." The girl takes a dramatic breath and says: "I didn't get accepted, but I don't think that was entirely Eugene's fault." She brushes a tear from her eye.

Oh, Eugene. What went wrong? I mean, besides everything.

Let's not listen to the next pretty girl on the podium, a colleague of Eugene's who summarizes a study she has been working on concerning tarantism, the overwhelming urge to banish one's melancholy by dancing. The dance she does is something else, though. With hardly a move, she manages to communicate depression and nakedness.

By the way, Eugene, I'm not one of those people who go around saying, "But if I had to do it all over again, I would."

The lights dim. I see a few people fuss about for their coats, the way you do when you think things are wrapping up at the theater and want to make sure you get a taxi. But then the slide show begins and there is no getting away unless you care to look as if you're walking out on Eugene. A gold art card appears that says: EUGENE OBELLO. Underneath the name were Greek numbers, but nobody sitting near me could figure out if they were his dates of birth and death or his phone number.

So, Eugene, you want to know what I would change? Last things first: for starters, there's the morning I showed up at the institute fit to be tied, which was just days before you kicked. How about this alternate sequence of events that I hope both of us can live with? Oh, sorry, Eugene.

It is hard for me to take my eyes off the slide show even though, or maybe because, it seems mainly to serve as photographic proof that Eugene stood next to several people of importance, some of whom have their arms wrapped collegially around him. I think my favorite is the montage of Eugene playing sports with the famous: See Eugene play tennis with the lieutenant governor of Kentucky. See Eugene water-ski with the greatest composer in Luxembourg. See Eugene miniature-golf with the ex-wife of the statesman responsible for bombing Vietnam.

Anyway, let's say that on that morning, you finally step out of your office, Eugene—but only to beeline through the waiting room. When you return, you say, "I was detained in the loo." Ick, I think.

"Can we talk?" I say, lowering my voice. You look nervous. We go to the faculty lounge. Spine stiffened by a Diet Coke from the vending machine, I brace myself and say, "Um, anything new?"

"Despite my domestic turmoil, kitten," you say, "I seem to be making remarkable breakthroughs in my research on the ways in which female hysteria is used as an aggressive strategy against the principled man." I interrupt you because this is the new me. "What about your nine o'clock? The isolophobe," I say with prosecutorial panache.

You put your hand on mine and I slither my hand away. See the new me, Eugene! The new me cannot be appeased by a hand stroke. The new me cannot be sweet-talked. The new me cannot be seduced by your smarts or by looking at me with your look. The new me will never again let you get away with telling me that I am the one, then disappearing for an interminable stretch. The new me is no chump. The new me is loaded with dignity and self-regard. The new me feels she deserves to be with someone with whom she has a future, not a past—maybe a mechanical engineer or a dermatologist.

"Sunny and I met under professional circumstances many months ago," you say. Professional circumstances! You are her fucking analyst and those are words chosen carefully. That is what I think, but I do not say this because even the new me has limits. "You would fancy her," you say and then massage my shoulder and the old me lets you. "Sunny has your sense of amuse-bouche,*" you say.*

Now, wait a minute. Nobody ever said my French is all that it could be, but it is plenty good enough for me to know that I do not want to be called a piece of food. Do you know what you're talking about, Eugene? For the first time, I wonder if you are such a big brain after all.

"Do you mean she and I are both amusant?" I say.

You acquit yourself as only you can. You lock your hand over mine and say, "I mean you are both fascinant."

A redheaded man who looks like a mouse approaches us. "Hey, Gene," he says. "You and Judy want to catch a movie tonight?"

Judy! Why it is that Judy and not Sunny, or for that matter, Margaret, prompts me to get up from the table, I cannot tell you. Maybe it is the realization that no matter how long I were to wait on the runway, there would always be another plane with clearance to take off before me. Or maybe the destination has ceased to look worth it.

I hear the lady in back of me say to the lady next to her, "This last one he was with, they said it was love at first sight. He took her to Venice when his wife was in the hospital having tests."

"He was a true romantic," comes the sincere reply. It is getting easier now for me to decathect from Eugene.

"Good riddance, Gene-yus!" I say to you and you are stunned. Yep. That's the way the past-its-sale-date cookie crumbled for you and me— but most irreparably, I guess, for you.

Margaret gives the final eulogy. One of the ushers offers her his arm on her way to the podium, but she sweeps him aside with courtesy. With her typical flair for color combination, Margaret has on a suit of deep maroon and charcoal gray with a baby blue shirt. "Thank you all for coming today to celebrate the life of my late and not-quite-ex husband," she says, and again come titters in the pews. "I see a few other Homeric scholars in the house and to you, I want to say that if Eugene was Odysseus in his long absences from home, I was never the loyal and patient Penelope whom most, but not all, academicians depict."

How has the round little man who'd been sitting next to Margaret and constantly blotting his forehead with a handkerchief taken Margaret's comment? I notice he is blowing his nose.

"But it is not my life we are celebrating," Margaret says with what could be discerned as a tinge of disappointment, "so I will leave it at that and say a few words about the father of my son." Perseus, I notice, is no longer in the pews.

"Toward the end of Eugene Obello's life," Margaret says, "he had developed an enviable commitment to his golf game." Margaret pauses to allow the snickering to subside. "But that, of course, wasn't all that we will remember about Eugene Obello," she says as she sets her fingers on the edge of the podium and leans in. "It was said that he also had a very deft touch when it came to quim. Perhaps some of you know what I mean." If anybody does know what she means, that person is not speaking up. There is silence. Margaret takes her hands off the podium—she seems now to have all the time in the world. She takes a deep breath and saunters to her seat. Incidentally, her remarks have been off the cuff. Sometimes, it takes a man to die for you to realize you should have liked his estranged wife better than you liked him.

"He was lucky to have her until he didn't," the lady in back of me says.

And that was the end of that. A lot of people find memorial services too maudlin, but in general, I don't find them maudlin enough. Except for Eugene's.

As the pews empty of the heartsick and the heart-well, you can hear the organist play a pretty swinging "Hit the Road, Jack." The receptionist files past me and shakes her head. It doesn't take much to make me nervous these days. "I'm sorry," I say, to cover past, present, and future transgressions.

"He wasn't for you, hon," she says and then she smiles.

Eugene's neighbor, the man who loves hymns, helps me on with my coat and introduces himself. When I introduce myself back, he smiles at the mention of my name and says, "Is it really you? Are you aware that Eugene used to gush about you all the time? And verily, I find you as enchanting as he claimed." Is this fellow soft-soaping me? Is he confusing me with someone else? Or had Eugene really talked about me to him? Now *that* would mean something, would it not? Try as I might, I cannot help but be won over.

THIRTEEN

Listen, there's a part I haven't told you. If you promise not to tell anyone this—not Margaret, not my parents, not Obax or Libby, or Corby or Sarah or Meg or Martha or Ann or any of those mourners at the Princeton University chapel—if you promise, I'll let you in on what really happened in the hours and days after the isolophobe walked out of Eugene's office that morning I was sitting there in the waiting room.

Objectively speaking, I could not blame the receptionist for trying to get rid of me. Then again: Is there any more moronic oxymoron than "objectively speaking"? Okay, yes, knocking incessantly on an analyst's door while screaming, "Let me in, you depraved jerkhole!" is probably against regulations, even in a place that caters to crackpots. But how, I wondered, could the receptionist have failed to understand that despite my carrying on, all I wanted was to sit down and have a respectful and well-mannered heart-to-heart with Eugene? And how could Eugene, who surely had heard the rumpus outside his door, not let me in? Unfortunately, I knew the answer to these questions.

Eventually, as I said, Eugene did open the door. He had no choice. There was the angry bulimic in the waiting room whose session was to have started a long time ago. You don't want to keep a patient waiting if you're in the mental-health-care industry because you'll have to spend the next fifty minutes talking about the meaning of the delay. The door opened slowly, just a smidgeon, and then stopped. It was not the way Eugene usually opened a door.

"Do you think we could talk?" I said to the part of Eugene I could see.

The receptionist pushed her way in front of me. "She says she knows you," she said to Eugene.

"I do know him!" I said. "I know him *very* well." For the record, it had become clear to me by then that in fact, I did not know Eugene at all.

The receptionist rolled her eyes. "Should I call the police, Dr. Obello?" she said. This from the woman who had led me to believe she was on my side. Hadn't she interrupted her Xeroxing to offer me water and then allowed me to help myself to the peppermint candies on the counter?

"That's a tad severe," Eugene said, coming out from behind the door. "Let's have a go at managing it ourselves, shall we?"

As he beckoned me into his office with a forefinger curl, the bulimic sprung into action. "It's my turn," she said and she, too, pushed her way between me and Eugene. "I'm an emergency!" she said. The bulimic maneuvered herself into Eugene's office. He followed her and shut the door but not entirely. I could hear Eugene placate the bulimic with the lure of a double session later that day. And then I could hear her negotiate a deal to make both hours on the fucking house and then she was on her merry way. As she passed through the waiting room, she took two ample handfuls of peppermint candies.

I slipped into Eugene's office before anyone else could beat me to it. The office was not what you or I would have expected: no dark wood panels; no midcentury pieces of furniture; no Oriental rugs; no spotlit paintings that required symbolic decoding; no receptacle for canes; no coat hook made from an elephant tusk; no footrest with ivory inlay; no collections of antique statuettes and totems; no bookshelves with first editions; no humidifiers for the statuettes and totems; no dehumidifiers for the first editions; no Pierre Boulez concertos in the background; no hundred-year-old port. This is what there was: furniture upholstered in shiny plaid fabric; a striped cloth rug that didn't match the plaid; a large sequined pillow on the floor; a colorful poster of a gigantic daisy; an urn with artificial flowers; a Yellow Pages; lots of diplomas; a trophy that seemed to be for excellence in golf; a pack of sugarless chewing gum. If this was Eugene's office, then I didn't know Eugene. But if I didn't know Eugene, who did I know?

Eugene stood in the doorway to his office. As he and the receptionist discussed the chances that he would be finished with work in time to attend the Depression Luncheon that day, Eugene motioned for me to sit in the armchair. Notice that he did not motion for me to sit on the couch—the couch on which, in my imagination at least, all sorts of monkey business had occurred with Eugene and the isolophobe as he was trying to help her overcome her isolation. I heard Eugene tell the receptionist that he was most sanguine that he could wrap up in time for the lunch. In other words, he wasn't planning to spend much time with me.

Eugene sat in a maroon vinyl desk chair. "Tell me how you

are feeling, my sweet delicate flower," he said and rolled toward me on his chair, using his feet to paddle himself along. Eugene leaned in and peered at me the way you might look at a three-legged dog in the pound. That look gave me the creeps.

"I'm fine," I said. Why start with the truth this late in the game? He's the shrink, let him try to see through the occlusive miasma of my dexterous obfuscations, I thought.

"Splendid!" Eugene said. "Because I absolutely could not endure your feeling wounded, my little bear."

Do you think it could have been the molecules coming out of the white-noise machine that were causing me to free-associate? Anyhow, I was reminded that Corby used to tell people that he had a job killing dogs for the city. The put-on would not have amused Eugene. Thinking about this made me smile, which made me worry that Eugene would think that I had softened toward him, which made me unsmile. On the other hand, I did not want to come across as wounded. So I smiled again, then toned it down to an insipid grin, which, I worried, could be taken as a sign of my being mentally defective, so I tried to affect an air of indifference, but afraid that that might translate as being bored, I grimaced, then simpered, then scowled, then pouted, then faked an oh-so-pensive expression, then attempted a poker face, which I suspected looked as if I were about to throw up, so I settled on a show of resignation until finally returning to the smile. I have always had a hard time knowing what to do with my face.

Eugene, meanwhile, was on the telephone. "*À bientôt,* my only one," I heard him say. I believe I may have glowered.

If the world can be divided into people who would have signed the Munich Agreement versus those who would have stood firm against Hitler—and who says it can't?—I would definitely have been in the former camp, giving away the Sudetenland with a smile and a cookie. I might even have offered the Führer a signing bonus, for example the mineral rights to South Dakota. As you know, I am not big on making trouble. But that morning, in Eugene's office, I had not been myself (which, in my case, is not generally but sometimes a very good thing not to be). And that is why, after Eugene said *à bientôt,* I stood up and said, "I think it is time to terminate."

At that point, I still had hoped for a nonfelonious solution, though I could not imagine what it could be. At that point, I still had thought there was a one in a million chance that it might have been Perseus on the other end of the line. At that point, I still had faith that Eugene could not turn his back on almost ten years of us. At that point, I still had believed I would somehow get around to finishing my thesis. At that point, I was still young. At that point, I had been about to march off in a huff but first I had to look under the armchair to see if that was maybe where I had misplaced my sunglasses.

At the next point, the receptionist knocked on the door and simultaneously stepped inside. She looked at me and said to Eugene with an edgy urgency, "Are you okay?" What had she been thinking? That I was down on the floor looking for a handgun? Of all the ways to knock someone off, shooting would not be my choice. I'm no good with mechanical things.

Eugene laughed. "Just a confabulation; that's all this is," he said to the receptionist. "We're old chums from school." The receptionist shrugged and walked out, returning, I suppose, to her Xeroxing.

At this point, I walked out, too. "You know what?" I said. "I can't stay. I'm late for something." How I wish my departure had been more resounding. How I wish I had come up with a more Shakespearean exit line, I mean, exeunt line. Plus, I never found my sunglasses.

At the doorway, I stopped long enough to hear Eugene say, "You mustn't be miffed, my one-of-a-kind. I was only trying to help a patient get through a rough patch."

Sunny, for that was the isolophobe's name, I eventually learned, was not the only one going through a rough patch. It's odd, isn't it, how patches come in patches? Is it that everyone is miserable at the same time, or is it that the sob story of one person begets the sob story of another person? A case of one-downsmanship. A keeping down with the Joneses thing.

Based on reports from friends and nonfriends, too, it was a time of being pickpocketed, feeling lumps, getting an abortion, not getting an abortion, not getting the most amazing job, feuding with officemates, being gypped out of the Christmas bonus, being driven crazy by the phone company, being outbid on the perfect apartment, losing health insurance, having floods in the basement, picking the wrong tiles, gaining six pounds, flunking out. Everywhere, girlfriends were delivering ultimatums, neighbors threatening to call the super, IRS agents auditing tax returns, mothers showing early signs of Alzheimer's, children scoring too low, houseguests staying too long, parakeets dying, cars breaking down, bicycles disappearing, ankles spraining, knees busting up, dissertations not being written, love not being reciprocated, dishwashers going on the fritz. Obax wrote to me from Somalia that her *crêperie* had been burglarized. Uncle Walt found out about Aunt Sugar's man and wanted a divorce. My mother thought she might need a bunion operation. Corby ran out of money and went back to Maine. Right about then, you probably weren't feeling so hot yourself.

But, tragically, at least in my opinion, misery does *not* love company. Misery likes to be the only one at the party. No, that's not it. Misery likes to be the only party girl who is miserable, for misery loves attention. And yet, misery does not feel that the company can ever truly understand what misery is going through. Well, that's how I felt.

The day after I found out about Sunny and swore off Eugene for good, a group of my sympathetic friends took me to lunch at a fancy French place where flowers were abundant. We split first courses and talked about makeup, hair, and because Cynthia was anxious about her dog that had an anxiety disorder, we also talked about our favorite prescription medicines. When the entrées came, my friends turned grave. "I'd like to make a toast," Phoebe said, holding up her glass, "to the last we'll ever hear of Eugene!" Hear, hear, everyone said.

"He's going to go bald," Nina said. "I can always tell."

"The one time I saw him," Joan said, "his pants were too short."

"And where were the cuffs?" Sarah said.

"No cuffs? Really? No cuffs on his pants, that is unacceptable," Esther said.

Buffy left early because of her plumbing disaster. The others followed suit shortly thereafter due to their respective crises. Susan was the last to leave. Dental trouble. Misery sipped her cappuccino alone.

My apartment was big and quiet and twice as much rent without Corby. I would have welcomed a tae kwon do kick or two in the living room. Isn't it interesting that all it takes is a catastrophe and you can start to miss the thing you hate most about someone? The only thing to do, it seemed, was to sell the Ben Shahn drawing I had inherited from my grandmother. The drawing was of some dockworkers who were either fighting or having their sandwiches; my family could never agree to which. So sell the drawing or get a job. And you know me.

"Be careful with this," my father had said when he gave me the drawing. "It depicts social injustice and it's very valuable. Don't expose it to sunlight." Out of respect, I did not remind him that my grandmother had kept the drawing in her sunroom.

"You know what's so great about art?" Uncle Walt had said to me when I told him I'd been given the drawing. "It appreciates."

I wrapped a towel around the drawing and took it to Sotheby's because everyone's heard of Sotheby's. But maybe everyone doesn't know that Sotheby's doesn't look very, um, Sotheby-an. I had wanted it to be a majestic old building on Park Avenue, but instead it was a dingy box of white bricks way over by the East River. The rug was wall-to-wall.

In the lobby, a guy wearing a uniform told me to sit down over there and wait while he located someone who could help me. Here's how long I waited: long enough to relive all the wonderful moments I'd had with Eugene and long enough to relive all the other kinds of moments I'd had with Eugene and long enough to tear the cuticles on two of my fingers and long enough for my Ben Shahn drawing to appreciate.

Every so often, another thin blonde in a pencil skirt and high heels flounced down the stairs and veered into a room off the lobby where I gathered from what was hysterically being said in passing that a major example of eighteenth-century French faience had been chipped. The blond numbers kept coming, one after the other, each more fraught-looking than the one before. Not to bring myself yet again into the middle of everything, but was anyone ever going to take notice of me me me? Finally a Miss Taffy Canal peeled off from the parade of blondes and asked if I had an appointment.

After all I'd been through, can you blame me for saying, "Yes, I believe I do"?

"Who are you affiliated with?" Miss Taffy Canal said.

I'm not even affiliated with myself, was what I thought. "The Walters Art Museum," I said because what the hell.

"We have an emergency with a tureen right now," Miss Taffy Canal said. "Can you come back another day?"

"I'm sorry," I said, "but this cannot wait." Have you ever said that before? Have you ever not given someone a way out? Because it works. And I'm pretty sure it doesn't just work on blondes. But now that I'm telling you this, I am wondering if Miss Taffy Canal might simply have wanted to make sure I was not going to do anything that would lead to more porcelain breakage.

Miss Taffy Canal ushered me into a small room far away from the faience. "I think you will agree," I said as I removed the towel from my inheritance, "that this is a very fine pictorialization of social injustice." I took a step back so as not to cast a shadow on any part of the pictorialization. Miss Taffy Canal took a look-see, as Eugene would have said. She did not, however, put her eye right up to the drawing, the way I thought experts were supposed to do.

"This is a print," explanation point, she said, as aghast as if I'd promised a Rembrandt and given her instead a plate of spaghetti. "It's worthless, worrrrrrrrrrrrrrrthless." That Miss Taffy Canal was not a specialist in twentieth-century American drawing, but rather in the tureen, did not make me feel any better about my inheritance.

From a list that included EZ Cash, Pawnderella, Pawn of a New Civilization, We Pay Lots, We Pay More, Lefty's, and Mr. Reasonable, I chose Honest Abe's Pawnshop on 148th Street. When I got there, a man, presumably Honest Abe, was being led away in handcuffs by three policemen.

On my way home, I thought I saw Eugene three times. I put on lipstick because, I figured, one of these days I was sure to see

Eugene. I will run into him when I least expect to (that is what I expect). There will be a piquant chill in the air. The sun will be setting in a way that flatters complexions. Eugene will emerge from the subway and he will look a little pale, despite the setting sun. The street will be still, traffic will be sparse, passersby few. A gust of wind will blow Eugene's school scarf off his neck and onto the pavement. He will stoop to pick it up, lingering down there to, what, catch his breath? He will see me when he straightens up and his face will brighten. He will hesitate, but then he will kiss me on the cheek. He will take a step back and gaze into my eyes. "You look smashing, my pined-for one," he will say.

"Oh, it's just the light," I will say. "And, of course, the piquant chill in the air." Then I will giggle coquettishly and say, "And don't forget the ever-so-still street."

"What are you doing now?" he will say. "Fancy a tea and some nibbles?"

And then a handsome man will walk briskly toward me—so handsome that Eugene will think he has maybe seen him in a movie or that the man is an important politician. The handsome man will give me a proprietary caress and say, "Sorry I'm late."

I will say to him, "This is Eugene Obello. We're old chums from school." Eugene will put his hands in his pockets. And he will look away. Can you believe it? I will feel sorry for Eugene.

It could have happened. But it did not happen that day on my way home.

Now what? I gave the Ben Shahn to my next-door neighbor and do you know what she said? "Was this mounted on an acid-free mat? If not, it's just going to fade, turn yellow, and eventually disintegrate and taint my other works of art." Disintegrate is the opposite of appreciate, I thought. But who cares? The drawing was worrrrrrrrrrrrrthless.

When I got back to my apartment, after the neighbor's dog had taken a bite out of me, there was a message on my machine from my mother. She was wondering, she said, when I was going to start my job in Minneapolis because Aunt Sugar had a guy she wanted me to meet there. He manufactured bra hooks. On top of everything, I cut my finger trying to open the Band-Aid box.

Now what? In the end, I am not, as you must have surmised, particularly Sylvia Plath–ish. In the beginning, maybe; but not the end. In the end, I want to be there to see how it ends. I want to know conclusively: Did Jane and Skip Hamblen stay married? Was I right about Glen being gay? Did Perry keep the weight off? Did Alice lose her looks? Which of my friends' children turned out best (and which turned out to be felons)? Had researchers really been on the verge of curing that rare disease? When all was said and done, did the terrorists win? What did the Dow finally do? In the end, can there be anything sadder than one's death? It is the single thing worth crying about.

If only, I thought, I could talk to Eugene just one more time. This was before I came to understand that you cannot make someone fall in love with you. But here's what you *can* do. By arguing and pleading and screaming and crying and throwing plates and phoning a lot and bringing hot food and sending flowers and buying gifts and doing unsolicited favors and remembering a birthday and being nice and declaring your abiding love and trying hard or sometimes merely by being present, you can make someone who was hitherto lukewarm really detest you.

To track down Eugene's new address, I called his receptionist. In a foreign accent of no known language, I said I was a dispatcher from the Sofa Shed and that I had two deliverymen in the field trying to deliver a love seat to a Mr. Eugene Obello.

So here's a tip: When you want to get anything done, use devious means.

That night, I showed up at Eugene's new bachelor pad. Needless to say, I came bearing no gift basket, no fragrant soaps, no "Bless This House" doorplate. I think Eugene might have been expecting someone because after I rang the bell, I could hear through the door, "What are you wearing, my ultimate creature?" Which would have made me the penultimate; I guess I could live with that.

The door opened promptly and there was Eugene, proffering a bottle of wine and turned out in a long puffy checked robe that made him look as if he'd been upholstered. Both the wine and the robe were open. Eugene did not look greatly pleased and, given my mood, who could blame him?

The only light came from a few candles on the mantel, but still, I could see that the room was full of cartons, unopened, I believe. I could also see two glasses of wine on a crate next to a sofa. I could hear sultry guitar music. I could smell incense. I could feel that it was a romantic scene minus the romance.

"What a treat, my uninvited angel," Eugene said. I noticed he did not budge from the doorway. Eugene clearly wants me to leave, I thought, so I guess I'll just stay—reasoning based on the hard-to-defend principle that once you lose a little pride, you might as well lose the whole pride shebang. Somehow, humiliation seemed my only way of gaining some dignity. Or could it be that I really wanted another round with Eugene, however stacked against me?

I squeezed past Eugene and made my way into the living room, where I stationed myself next to a freestanding and highly designed metal floor-to-ceiling bookshelf that was crammed mostly with disarrayed stacks of books but also a few odd items that I assume were waiting for further placement—a crystal vase, a pair of scissors, two telephones, a radio, a pair of candlesticks, a flute, a framed photo of Eugene and someone in a bikini, and so forth. Eugene had followed me into the living room, but stood his distance. "I just took a tub," he said. "I was about to retire for the night."

If that was supposed to be a hint for me to leave, I did not take it. Eugene looked toward his bedroom. "Excuse me, my nocturnal apparition," Eugene said, "while I put on some slippers." He shivered, but it looked kind of fake. "Brrrr," he said. "I shan't be but a moment."

The moment seemed quite an extended one. That's when I started to daydream about what it would be like if Eugene were retired permanently. How perhaps his heart would give out in the middle of doing it with some nymphet in Central Park, how nobody would have anything very tender to say at the funeral, how I would not have to write a condolence note to anyone since Margaret would be in no need of consoling and Eugene's parents, I assumed, had no idea who I was, though I had spoken to his mother once on the phone years ago. But flirting with notions of Eugene's demise was, sadly, not the tonic I'd hoped it would be. Because imagination can take you only so far. Because after I imagined the worst for Eugene, there he still was, with heart strong and me-less future bright.

"Perhaps we might continue our tête-à-tête at a later date," Eugene said, "for all at once I'm feeling a touch fluey." He cupped his hand on my elbow, trying to nudge me toward the door. "Come," he said, but he meant "go."

"Just tell me this," I said, refusing to be nudged. "I'm curious about something." I picked up one of the glasses of wine on the crate, although, you might remember, I don't drink. The music came to a stop. Then I couldn't remember what it was I wanted to know.

"As I tell my patients," Eugene said, "it's much harder to feel sad than it is to feel mad." He picked up the flute from the bookcase and blew a few notes. I didn't know he played and based on what I heard, it could be argued that he did not. "Try just to feel sad," Eugene said. "Can you do that, my downcast dove?" He played some sad music.

I didn't say anything. I watched Eugene put down the flute and survey a pile of books, pulling out a copy of Nietzsche's *Beyond Good and Evil*. This was a book I recognized well because I had once written a term paper called "Whither Nietzsche? Thus Spake I." I felt no need to tell Eugene about the coincidence.

Eugene looked up from the book. "Whatever happens," he said, "I will always feel a great deal of agape toward you, O my everlasting."

Not so O everlasting. I decided to get out of there, though once again, I had nothing cute in the way of an exit line. "I know what the word 'agape' means," I said, but in a voice so faint, I do not think Eugene could have heard. I and the glass of wine headed toward the bookcase, where I had set down my pocketbook. Gripping his hand around my wrist, Eugene said, "I hope someday we will be able to laugh about this, my enduring comrade."

Guess what? I would say to Eugene today if I could. That day has come! Here are the people I have laughed about it with: Lisa, Deb, Meg, Joan, Pearson, Susan, Phil, Buffy, Cynthia, Larry, Mark, Jeff, Martha, Phoebe, Sarah, Nina, Ann, Anne, and Esther; Johnny Cake; vogueish Rebecca; Samantha Martin; Suzanne Balaban; Katie Monaghan; Madeleine Stoner; Clarky Sonnenfeld; the Rakoff brothers; the Galen sisters; Nino at the Philadelphian . . .

Just a moment. As you might have deduced, this is the section in which the author thanks the many people who have helped in the writing of this book. If you do not know the author, I fear you may be uninterested and advise you to hurry on a few pages until the end of the next paragraph. On the other hand, there is a chance that you may be mentioned, perhaps in a coded fashion, so think twice before skipping ahead.

. . . Gordo Lish (twice or maybe three times); the perfect David del Gaizo (who understood the first time); Zora Chast (who was laughing so hard she choked on her milk); D. Avedon (did you know him? you would have *loved* him!); Baby Lizzie Kastenmeier, who was too young to talk, but seemed to coo with understanding and even, I think, with sympathy (whereas the Blattstein baby threw up); Nell Minnow, who asked if I'd sell her the movie rights; Nancy C.; Laura and Jay S-K; Howdie Iselin; Less Simplyrich; Lady Duenwald; Nolan Tobias, Nolan Tobias II, and Nolan Tobias III; my optometrist, Miss Carey, but not my optician, Dr. Sandy; Sally, who washes my hair at the Stuart Salon, but not Charlie, the man who cuts my hair; the varsity volleyball team at Sheanshang High; David Evangelista and everyone at his pool party; R. Bernstein, who owns a fantastic vintage store in Los Angeles (no relation to J. Bernstein, whom I also told); Owen Hodge (the man who teaches small animals to play golf); everyone I met on jury duty including Judge Doumanian; the Amazing Dietzo; S. Morrison, who is really the talk of the town; the McCalls, who drove to Luxembourg; Dylan Joseph the D-man; S. Becker of the Harold Agency; Alexandra and Alessandra and the Andersens (but not Alessandro because he was away); the Lewis/Lacey family, including cousins; all the Pepalls; Adam the waffle maker at Madison Fine Foods; a Russian boxer named Nemrick or Renmick or something; the Barrett-Lethems, whom I sat with on the blue hill; Father Panick, whom I'd met on the street while he was asking people to sign a petition against God; the New York Stringfield-Martins, the California Martin-Stringfields, and the omnipresent Wally; the lady in my building who machine-washes

her entire wardrobe every day; Enilk Nivek, the nice newsstand
man on Ninety-fourth; a homeless guy; Nadine Stine, who has
since passed away; Minnie Stine, who is still with us; some bitter
woman in the ladies' room who wanted to know where she could
buy metal bookcases and how far away from them her husband
the bastard should stand; the handyman in my building while he
was unclogging the drain in my bathtub; my gynecologist while
I was getting a Pap smear; the mayor of Hoboken, New Jersey,
while I was stuck on an elevator; Janny during breakfast; the
Borowitzes the day before the thing happened; my friend Penny's
daughter, Lee (I was baby-sitting); Eliza Martin, whom I met in
the dilating room at the eye doctors; Kreahfried, the locksmith
who destroyed my door when I lost my keys; most of the guests
at Ann Yih's paella party; the weekend staff of the Hempel dog-
walking agency; the members of Wildfire (via e-mail); the brilliant, handsome, and downright perfect Paul Roossin, who's
helped me with so much, including writing this sentence; Sarah
McGrath, with whom I will be having lunch today and whom I
will be thanking for everything she's done, and believe me, it was
a lot; Nan Graham, who is not only a super editor but almost an
anagram for "anagram," too!; my agent and friend, Esther Newberg (where would I be without Esther Newberg?); Corby, who,
the day after I called to tell him, drove down from Maine with a
bucket of steamers, which we threw at each other for old times'
sake; Obax, who said she wished Etienne had suffered the same
fate; Libby, who was in the middle of divorcing her husband and
wrote to ask whether I thought we'd be better off switching to les-
bianism; Frick Rips, who was working for a supermarket magazine in Florida and wanted to know if he could write about
Eugene and also if it would be all right to tell the story to Joyce
Slutzky, who had left TV and was now married to Dwayne
Schmokler's oral surgeon, and also if I wouldn't mind if he told

her parrot, Grover; Polly Bean (and since Arnie Bean, my parents
have come to suspect, had been working in London for the CIA
and not the Lumb hamburger chain, there is a possibility that
Eugene is now being laughed about at a top-secret level, too);
Aunt Sugar, whom I told not to tell anyone because I wanted to
make sure she told everyone; my mother, who said she never liked
Eugene even though I know she had; my father, who said, "What
kind of kooky name is Obello, anyway?" I also sent a report of
Eugene's decease, including a list of some of the women "he leaves
behind," to his class secretary at the *Princeton Alumni Weekly*. The
news item appeared in print the next week.

I laughed with so many people about Eugene, I do not have time
to mention them all. And now I have laughed about him with you.

I freed my wrist from Eugene's hold.

It could have been the extra weight of the glass of wine I put
down on the bookshelf or it could have been the swing of my
pocketbook into one of the stacks of books as I took a step away
or it could have been an engineering flaw or it could have been
the way in which Eugene stumbled briefly and knocked against
the center divider or it could have been the vibrations emanat-
ing from the subway that ran underneath the apartment or it
could have been the sonic reverberations of the word "agape"
or it could have been a change in barometric pressure or it could
have been bad luck or it could have been good luck or it could
have perhaps been that firm little yank I purposefully exerted on
the side panel, but whatever it was, it did it.

The bookcase was teetering.

I saw it.

During those moments, as the bookcase swayed to and fro, I might have rushed in heroically to act as his shield or pull him free from the inevitable. I might have at least said, "Look out, my endangered species!" But it might have been in vain. If my grandmother had been right that everyone has a fixed number of steps to take, it is possible that Eugene had taken his.

It was this and that and that and this until finally it was pieces of wood, shards of glass, crushed metal, book spines, torn paper, and Eugene all over the place—until finally it was some heap of a mess.

They always say you're in shock when this kind of thing happens. And maybe I was. But didn't somebody have to do something about Eugene and don't you hate it when that somebody turns out to be you? Calling Margaret never occurred to me. For some reason, calling 911 didn't occur to me, either, and obviously it wasn't because I didn't have the number. As I stood there, waiting patiently for an idea, the doorbell rang.

I said excuse me to what remained of Eugene and ran. I heard a clock somewhere strike eleven. At the door was Eugene's nine o'clock, the isolophobe. Eugene never did find out what she was wearing but you can: a flowered baby-doll dress and red high heels. Never was I as grateful to see someone I couldn't stand.

I don't know what happened next, but the isolophobe must have made some calls because soon there was an ambulance and professionals took over or so I'd heard someone say at the service. According to the autopsy, the thing that killed him was a copy of *The Psychopathology of Everyday Life* (I think he would have been happy about that serendipity), which had rammed into his neck and freakishly cut off his breathing.

You know what my immediate thought was? That I had to tell my parents right away I did not get a job in Minneapolis, Pittsburgh, or Detroit.

The End

Want to know what happened next? Some people think I must have wound up in trouble with the law. Or maybe they wished I had. I'm thinking of the people—I hope not you—who seem to think I had done something wrong. Like murdering. The funny thing is that these are the same people who'd disapproved of me for having had anything to do with Eugene, especially once he was married. (Wouldn't you think these would be the people who'd be applauding the death of Eugene, however it came about?)

There is only so much that can be said in one's defense.

But let me tell you what took place after the isolophobe had called for help. I'll spare you the awkward chitchat between the isolophobe and me while we waited for the ambulance, but I will tell you that she complimented me on my shoes.

Two paramedics sped in with lots of machinery and pronounced Eugene dead. I admit he didn't look his usual self, but he didn't look dead, either. Breathing can be very subtle. Eugene's robe was disarranged and one of his slippers had come off, but neither the isolophobe nor I did anything about it. I can't speak for her, but I was afraid of fingerprints.

Then two police officers arrived. Don't ask me why everyone was coming and going in pairs that night. Eugene, with his "Philosophy of the Number Two," probably would have gotten a chuckle out of that. Anyway, one of the guys "interviewed" me and the other, the isolophobe. While that was going on, the paramedics took a lot of measurements with their machines. My cop asked certain questions that I didn't want to answer.

I went home and slept for ten hours.

I think this is where I'll end. Stories have to end somewhere.

One more thing. The guys who had installed the bookcases said that Eugene had written them a note asking that nails not be used to attach the metal to the ceiling because that would "compromise the integrity and poetry of the unit, my able artisans." They used high-strength suction cups. Enough said?

Appendices

APPENDIX A

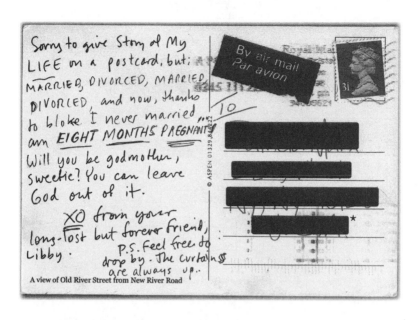

Sorry to give Story of My LIFE on a postcard, but; MARRIED, DIVORCED, MARRIED, DIVORCED, and now, thanks to bloke I never married, am EIGHT MONTHS PREGNANT! Will you be godmother, sweetie? You can leave God out of it.

XO from your long-lost but forever friend, Libby.

P.S. Feel free to drop by. The curtains are always up.

A view of Old River Street from New River Road

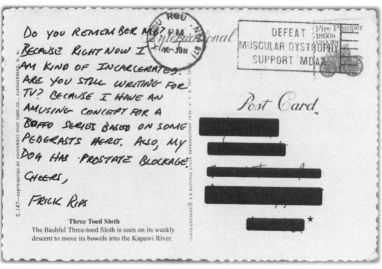

DO YOU REMEMBER ME? BECAUSE RIGHT NOW I AM KIND OF INCARCERATED. ARE YOU STILL WRITING FOR TV? BECAUSE I HAVE AN AMUSING CONCEPT FOR A BOFFO SERIES BASED ON SOME PEDERASTS HERE. ALSO, MY DOG HAS PROSTATE BLOCKAGE.

CHEERS,

FRICK RIPS

Three Toed Sloth
The Bashful Three-toed Sloth is seen on its weekly descent to move its bowels into the Kapawi River.

* Editor's Note: Information withheld at the request of the narrator.

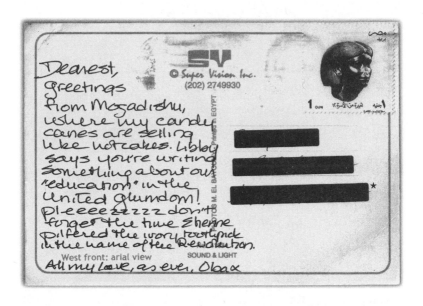

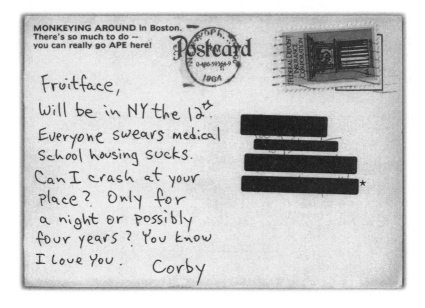

* Editor's Note: Information withheld at the request of the narrator.

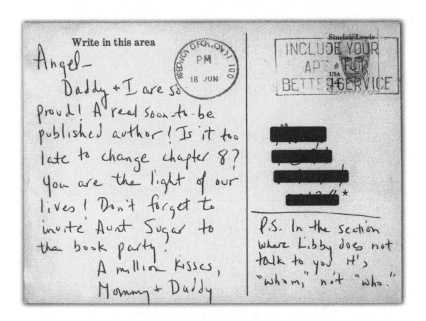

Write in this area

Angel—
  Daddy + I are so
proud! A real soon-to-be
published author! Is it too
late to change chapter 8?
You are the light of our
lives! Don't forget to
invite Aunt Sugar to
the book party!
    A million kisses,
    Mommy + Daddy

PM
18 JUN

Sinclair Lewis
INCLUDE YOUR
APT #
BETTE 746 SERVICE
USA

P.S. In the section
where Libby does not
talk to you it's
"whom," not "who."

Joyce Slutsky has moved!

She is no longer a resident of the Fresh Horizons
Rehabilitation Clinic.   Her new address is:

Joyce Slutsky
c/o The Hon. Prince Vrydkrejgdj of Belarus
35 Voronjanskogo Str.
Minsk 74
220 074 Belarus

If the Republic fails, Leonid is
2nd in line to rule...
  keep your fingers crossed!

* Editor's Note: Information withheld at the request of the narrator.

APPENDIX B

Q & A WITH PATTY MARX

When you wrote this book, did the characters take over?

It would have been helpful, but alack (as "Eugene" might say), the characters in my book were too lazy for that. I had to do all the work myself.

Whom is Eugene Obello based on?

Hmm. I like that; the accusative case. My interrogator is taking over.

Cut it out. Did you model Eugene on anyone, because I think he went out with my cousin?

How come you people always think writers copy your relatives? I was, as it turned out, in one of my creative moods and made Eugene up, though now I'm wishing I'd based him on a real person because I've been told that the best thing that can happen to a book is a lawsuit.

What do you think is the most important part of writing?

Could you rephrase the question?

Thing what you important the writing of part is most do?

Well, a lot of famous writers and writing teachers will tell you that great writing is a matter of originality, point of view, or poetry of language. What I pay the most attention to, however, is word count.

Has anyone ever compared you with Dorothy Parker?

My work has been compared with that of Cervantes, Milton, Céline, Lorca, Robbe-Grillet, Pessoa, and late Salinger.

How does your word count measure up to that of Dorothy Parker's?
I think I see where you are headed with that question.

What writers have influenced you?
Plato and James Joyce, though not in person.

Are you the same Patricia Marx who is married to Daniel Ellsberg?
Next question.

Is it true that professional writers regard the letter G as a lame device—almost a crutch?
It's a little more complicated than that.

Have you ever had writer's block?
Well, you know what they say about that . . .

No. What do they say?
I thought you knew.

Do you write at a certain time of the day?
What time do you have?

Two thirty.
I never write at two thirty.

I heard that you and Harold Bloom have the same dog. Could you comment on that?
What makes you think that I would share a dog with a critic?

Where do you get your ideas?
Textiles.

APPENDIX C

Bisacca, Cohan, Cohan, and Bisacca, LLP
550 Park Avenue
New York, New York 10021

Dear Mr. Seidenberg-Spinell;

It was nice to speak with you the other day regarding your concerns about certain aspects of my book. You recommended that I make a few changes to the manuscript to guard against problems down the road, such as a court injunction against publication. I think you said (if my notes are correct!) that you were worried I may have crossed some lines—and possibly violated the Comstock Laws—as far as "libel, plagiarism, obscenity, and causing irreparable harm to the defense of the United States." I assume I'm in the clear when it comes to treason, right?

Below are some edits. I hope they do the trick.

On page 19, I had written that Libby liked to fool around with underage choir boys. You said that even though Libby is an entirely fictional character, someone real whose name is Libby might be offended. What if I change "Libby" here to "Secretary-General U Thant"? He's dead.

On page 63, I quoted 734 words from a book called *Shutterbabe* by Deborah Copaken Kogan, except—for artistic reasons—I didn't use quotation marks. I think you felt uneasy about this because maybe it constituted plagiarism or something. How about if I change the quote to one by Eleanor Roosevelt? Again: dead.

Page 104. What's so lewd about that?

Page 131. Let's take out the part about Bunsen burners in that case.

Page 16, page 30, and page 84. I think you know how I feel about character descriptions, but if you insist, I will provide some details about Eugene, Margaret, and Mr. Softie that will differentiate them, respectively, from your father, the speech therapist at your son's school, and your ex-wife's dog. First, Eugene. He is really, really tall—too tall, if you ask me. His mouth looks like the kind of pasta with a name I can never remember, but you probably never order it. Margaret has that dotty type of freckles I wish I had and please don't make me tell you any more about her. Mr. Softie's a dog; what can I say?

This, I believe, addresses all of the legal issues you have with the manuscript. I hope we don't have to change the date of publication because I have already sent out invitations to the launch party.

Sincerely,
"Your favorite author" (!)

ABOUT THE AUTHOR

PATRICIA MARX was the first woman to write for the *Harvard Lampoon* and has since published in *The New Yorker, The Atlantic Monthly, The New York Times, Vogue, Time* magazine, and *Spy.* She is a contributing editor to *Time* magazine. She was a staff writer for *Saturday Night Live,* and has written for *Rugrats* and many other TV shows. She has also written several screenplays and a number of books, including a series of children's books illustrated by *New Yorker* cartoonist Roz Chast *(Now Everybody Really Hates Me; Now I Will Never Leave the Dinner Table; Meet My Staff),* and humor books such as *How to Regain Your Virginity, The Skinny,* and *1003 Great Things About Getting Older.* She teaches sketch comedy at New York University.